His first volley . . .

of five shots took down two of the three men in the lead rank. The third had opened fire at the pillar just as Carter heaved the gas bomb well past the first group, aiming for the second set of three rifle-wielding men.

And then, as though the lobbing of the gas bomb had been some kind of signal, shutters began to open up all over the place, up and down the street.

The ambush was in full tilt now and Carter, as the target, did not see how it could possibly fail. . . .

NICK CARTER IS IT!

FROM THE NICK CARTER
KILLMASTER SERIES

NICK CARTER

KILLMASTER

THE ASSASSIN CONVENTION

CHARTER BOOKS, NEW YORK

THE ASSASSIN CONVENTION

A Charter Book/published by arrangement with
The Condé Nast Publications, Inc.

PRINTING HISTORY
Charter edition/September 1985

ISBN: 0-441-03211-7

Charter Books are published by The Berkley Publishing Group,
200 Madison Avenue, New York, New York 10016.
PRINTED IN THE UNITED STATES OF AMERICA

Dedicated to the men of the
Secret Services of the
United States of America

THE ASSASSIN CONVENTION

ONE

The really funny part was that Nick Carter was actually looking forward to his meeting with Raina Missou, even though the golden-skinned woman had come within a hair's breadth of blowing out his brains the last time he saw her. Checking his weapons more out of habit than wariness, he walked up the narrow, steep street, right into the heart of Tangier's infamous Casbah.

It was exactly three o'clock in the morning. The souk's stalls and shops had long since closed for the night. The two- and three-story whitewashed stucco buildings on either side of the winding street were dark. The shutters were drawn, of course, but a trained eye could always catch a gleam of light behind a shutter if it existed.

But Carter saw no light behind the shutters of the closed apartments along the crooked, ever-climbing Casbah street.

1

Suddenly he sensed movement ahead, behind an empty vegetable cart chained to a wrought-iron grille over a window. The street was dark, lit only by a few very dim streetlights, and someone moving behind the cart cast a shadow across the cobblestone street.

Carter stopped and checked his weapons again. His 9mm Luger, Wilhelmina, was snug in its holster under his left arm. His trusty stiletto, nicknamed Hugo, was in its sheath, strapped to his right forearm. Pierre, a small gas bomb, was taped to the inside of his upper thigh.

Since Carter didn't want light to suddenly appear behind all those closed shutters, he ignored the Luger and activated the mechanism that snapped the stiletto into his hand. He ducked inside a doorway, easing his body out of sight of anyone who might be behind that empty cart ahead, and waited, the razor-sharp blade tight in his palm. He noticed that the streetlight nearest the cart had no bulb.

Carter stood in the doorway, watching and listening. During the day, the crooked street would echo with the cries of vendors and shoppers and children, but now there was not so much as a sigh from the heart of the Casbah. There was only the soft breathing of the man named Nick Carter and, ahead, the almost imperceptible movement of a shadow on the cobblestones.

The Killmaster checked his watch and saw that he was late for his meeting with Raina. He had met Raina Missou, a stunning woman whose ancestry was part Spanish, part Moroccan, and part Chinese, five years earlier in Casablanca. In the course of an assignment, Carter had killed her drug-dealing gangster father, and Raina had vowed revenge. She had attempted to murder the AXE agent, but was arrested by Moroccan authorities, tried, and sentenced to life imprisonment.

A week ago, Carter was informed by David Hawk, head of AXE, that Raina had escaped and had used highly advanced computer equipment to send a message to Carter through AXE's main terminal. Two days before, Carter stood in Hawk's office in the Amalgamated Press and Wire Services Building on Dupont Circle in Washington, D.C.—Amalgamated was AXE's worldwide cover organization—and read the printout of the message:

> Sophisticated equipment now being installed to tap NATO's computers. Purpose: Elimination of cruise and all nuclear-capability missiles now deployed or to be deployed in Western Europe. Do not take this warning lightly. Will provide details only in person. Come to Restaurant Maroc in downtown Tangier. You will be contacted only if you say to the headwaiter, "No tip today. I'm a bit short on cash." Say this in French and then proceed to tip the headwaiter one hundred dollars in American money.

Hawk sent an almost lethal cloud of cigar smoke across his desk, then looked intently at his finest agent. "Hell, Nick, there's no way anybody with a computer can mess up NATO and its plans, no matter how sophisticated the equipment. This is obviously a ruse so she can get her hands on you again. She's still smarting, understandably, over her failure to kill you, and I imagine five years in a stinking Moroccan prison hasn't exactly endeared you to her. Your story against her was airtight."

Carter was reminded of the week he had once spent in a North African prison during a mission. The grinning rats were only part of the miserable conditions. Cockroaches the size and ferocity of scorpions were everywhere. Carter slept on a steel slab that was better than the floor only because it was dry. The food was so foul that he actually thanked his guard, who never spoke to him, for bringing him so little of it.

He'd had time to think in that jail. And he'd had time to work up a tremendous hatred for those responsible for his incarceration. He had a pretty good idea of just what had gone through Raina Missou's mind during the five years she was in prison.

Even so, they couldn't take a chance.

If some clever international hacker could tap into NATO's computers, there was no end to the potentially deadly mischief a military—or even a nonmilitary—mind could cause.

Nick Carter had gone to the Restaurant Maroc, delivered his little speech in French to the headwaiter, and slipped the man a hundred-dollar bill. The man looked Carter up and down, held the money up to the light to inspect it, just to make sure it wasn't counterfeit, then led Carter to a window table overlooking the spectacular sweep of the harbor.

Carter waited an hour, watching the door and wondering if the beautiful, dark-haired Raina would come into the restaurant, although he knew deep down that this was the first of several places he'd be sent to before he actually came face to face with the exotic woman who had nearly killed him.

THE ASSASSIN CONVENTION

Her messenger was a swarthy little Arab who walked sideways, like a crab. Carter guessed that the unusual gait stemmed from some wound, possibly a knifing in the groin. If so, the man had adapted admirably to his handicap. He moved like the wind, and was in and out of the restaurant in a matter of seconds—even before the arrogant headwaiter knew he was there.

Carter read the note Crabman had delivered. He was right. It sent him to a hotel lobby on the other side of the city where he was given another message that dispatched him to a sleazy nightclub where another message sent him to a spot on the highway toward Rabat. There, a limousine waited for him.

It was the message received there on the highway that sent Carter back into the city and up into the labyrinthine streets, alleys, and byways of the Casbah.

And now, up ahead no more than fifty yards, someone lay waiting for him. Perhaps it was a thief working the after-hours shift. Perhaps it was merely one of Tangier's army of homeless beggars rearranging his sleeping area under the cart and no threat at all.

Or again, perhaps it was part of an ambush set up by Raina Missou to make certain that Nick Carter didn't escape her bullet this time.

Carter checked his watch again. It was almost three-thirty. He had been dogging it in the doorway for the better part of a half hour. If an ambush lay ahead, he figured he'd given his would-be attackers enough time to get curious and itchy-fingered, and to come out of hiding to see if their quarry were still around.

But these people would be professionals, Carter

realized. Raina had tried the amateur route once, and it cost her five years of her life. She would have professional killers waiting for him on this dark street. In fact, the more he thought of that bulbless streetlight, the more he became convinced that it was part of the trap. He'd be walking out in the dim light into total darkness. The men up ahead, accustomed to the darkness, would have their night vision working for them.

Easy as shooting fish in a barrel. And he'd be the fish.

Carter was just easing out around the doorframe to get a peek at the empty cart where he had seen the shadow, when the street exploded in sound and light.

Someone had fired a flare gun straight down the street. The phosphorus shell left a streak of light, then slammed into the side of a stone building, exploding like a thousand Roman candles. The sky above the Casbah lit up.

And then three men carrying AK-47 rifles stepped from behind the cart and followed the trail of light toward where Nick Carter was hiding. Only his gas bomb was a suitable weapon against those three automatic rifles, but Carter doubted he'd have enough time to get it before they opened up.

Even as he thought that, three more men rose from behind the cart and followed the first three. These also carried AK-47s.

Carter bought time by whipping out Wilhelmina. As he aimed and fired with his right hand, he unzipped his fly and went for the gas bomb with his left. His first volley of five shots took down two of the three in the lead group. The third man had opened fire on the doorway just as Carter heaved Pierre well past the bodies of the two from the first trio, aiming for the second set of three rifle-wielding men.

And then, as though the lobbing of the gas bomb had been some kind of signal, shutters began to open up all over the place, up and down the steep street.

From the dark windows came a steady, withering, and considerably lethal outpouring of lead and copper and steel, and long tongues of crimson and orange flame.

All of it aimed at Nick Carter.

TWO

Carter knew that he could not win this battle against so many automatic rifles, not with the meager weaponry he carried. Even as the first volley was building up a head of steam, Carter had holstered Wilhelmina and was looking for a route of escape.

Most of the firing seemed to be coming from across the street. But Carter saw that shutters had been opened above him and saw the snouts of AK-47 rifles poking out over his head. There were men positioned on both sides, just in case their target should make a run for it.

Carter looked behind him and saw a door with a decorative grille on it. It was partially concealed from the street by a recessed doorway. He went down the three steps and tried the latch. Locked. Carter unleathered the Luger and, while the street still raged with hails of automatic rifle fire and bullets whined around him on the pavement, blew the latch to pieces.

The boom of the Luger was little more than a pop in the cacaphony of sound in the dark night. Just as a concentrated shower of copper-sheathed bullets tore into the plastered doorway above and behind him, Carter kicked open the door and went inside.

It was a bakery. He slammed the door and pushed a heavy wooden bench against it. His eyes, already acclimated to the dim light of the street outside, took only a few seconds to achieve full night vision. He saw the door leading to the kitchen where a huge oven stood, cold and lonely, and he saw stairs that led to a second-floor door.

The killer assigned to this building, Carter guessed, had either come over the roof or was a friend of the baker. Or it might even be the baker himself. Maybe there was more money to be made taking pot shots at someone from an upstairs window than there was in making the round flat loaves that passed for bread in Morocco.

But Carter was wrong about the baker. When he opened the door at the top of the stairs and went down the narrow hallway, he found the fat baker and his even fatter wife tied up in bed.

Carter found the hired gunman in the next room down the hallway. The man sat at the open window, his automatic rifle resting on the sill. He leaned out from time to time to see what was going on down below. Carter snapped the stiletto into his right palm, gripped the smooth hilt, and moved across the room like a breath of air, quiet as an idle thought.

There was no sound, not even when he drew the glistening blade of the slim knife across the gunman's throat. He hastily drew the man into the room to let the blood gush onto the floor and not out the window. Then he took the man's place and watched the street.

Tongues of flame licked from five windows across the narrow street. The five men there were still firing at the general area of the doorway leading to the bakery, as though programmed like robots to continue firing at one location until ordered otherwise.

Two men lay dead on the street several yards up the hill. Beyond them, the second trio of rifle-toting goons who had come out from behind the cart lay in the grotesque positions of an agonizing death. Pierre had been thorough.

Carter wondered about the sole survivor of the first group, and then he saw a burst of fire from a ground-level doorway across the street. The man had run there when Carter had first opened up with the Luger. Carter took careful aim, shielding Wilhelmina's muzzle to keep flame from showing, and picked off the gunman.

By leaning out the window, Carter saw that four other windows on his side of the street contained gunmen with automatic rifles. They sat at their positions, apparently ordered to watch for their prey to dash foolishly into the street.

Well, Carter thought with a grim smile in the dark room above the bakery, *at least the odds are a little better now*. Sixteen men had formed the original ambush; now there were only nine. Of those, five were blasting away their ammunition and four were waiting for the chance to waste their bullets as well.

It was obvious to Carter that the ambush could have succeeded only if the target happened to be new at the game, or thoroughly stupid, or both. The target had even been warned of the ambush by one man who had not been able to contain his curiosity and had moved just enough to look down the street, sending a shadow across the cobblestones.

If Raina Missou had arranged this little ambush, Carter mused, she was either slipping, or she didn't really want Carter killed. Not now, anyway. Then again, perhaps she thought there would be success in numbers. Sixteen men with automatic rifles should not fail to bring down a solitary and unsuspecting target, even a seasoned veteran.

Carter figured he had two choices. One was to wait until the men across the way ran out of ammunition and a search was begun by the men on his side. The second was to let the men across the street keep wasting bullets while he took out the men on his side, those with plenty of firepower left.

Carter left the rifle in the window, just in case one of the automatons across the street happened to look that way, and stepped over the body of the dead man. The blood was now oozing slowly from the wide gash in the man's throat, soaking into the frayed carpet of the little parlor. Carter walked around the bloody carpet and went into the hallway.

He found the staircase to the roof and went up. When he reached the roof, he heard sirens and knew that he would be spared the chore of disposing of the four gunmen on his side of the street. The Tangier police had finally gotten around to action.

Carter moved across an adjoining roof and dropped down to the adjacent street. He walked uphill, keeping to the shadows, until the street ended, then circled back to the street with the cart and the bakery. The firing had stopped. The street was filled with the flashing red lights of police cars and ambulances. During his career with AXE, Nick Carter had often found himself on the fringes of scenes like this, watching as men in white uniforms cleaned up the bloody aftermath of a gun battle. Sometimes he'd been the instigator, sometimes the intended victim.

He found the address he'd been given near the top of the hill where the street circled back: 991 rue Vicenza. Beyond the building was a high stone wall topped by an iron spike fence thick with vegetation. Carter knew that the rich of Tangier lived up there, looking down their aristocratic noses at the maze that was the Casbah.

Carter didn't want to walk directly in front of the small building to check its shuttered windows. He found a small vegetable stall across the street and jimmied the lock on the back entrance with his stiletto. He eased himself inside and, peering through cracks in the ancient boards, surveyed the two-story stone and brick building.

All the shutters were closed, and there was a dim light in a central entryway and corridor. Carter studied each window through a cupped hand, bending his fingers in such a way that a tiny opening was left at the far edge of his curved palm. It was like looking through a telescope the wrong way, but it had the effect of cutting out all extraneous light and allowing his eye to be far more sensitive to any light that might be coming from behind a shutter.

In time, he found that only one apartment in the building had its lights on. It was a corner apartment on the second floor, within inches of the high wall. Carter left the vegetable stall and eased through shadows to the wall, then crossed to Number 991.

The wall was easy to scale. Ancient and worn with time and the elements, the badly mortared stones were almost like steps. He crawled, using hands and feet, to the second-floor level and slipped onto a ledge between the wall and the building. The space was so narrow that, as he edged along toward a side window of the house, his chest scraped the wall.

He reached the window and found the shutters locked. He used the stiletto to pry loose one slat and peered into the apartment. He was looking into a living room where a lighted lamp sat on an ornate round table beside a shabby French provincial couch. The walls, covered by flowered wallpaper that had once been garishly mutlicolored but was now faded, were decorated with cheaply framed prints of famous paintings. There were three other chairs and several other pieces of ornate furniture in the room, but no people. Through a doorway, Carter could see part of the bedroom; through another, part of a tiny kitchen.

He hunkered down on the wall and kept his eyes glued to the space he'd created in the shutters. Nothing. After fifteen minutes his muscles began to cramp, and he wasn't learning anything new. If there were someone hiding in the apartment, he—or she—could remain in the bedroom, and this waiting game could go on and on.

Carter decided to move, and he eased back through the darkness, pressing against the rough stones and feeling his way back down. At the rear of the building, he descended to ground level and checked the back door. It was locked, and he could see light from inside through a slit along the bottom of the door. He jimmied the lock with Hugo and opened the door. It was silent as the grave. He closed the door carefully and went inside. He pressed back into a corner and watched the short empty corridor that ran all the way to the glass front door. A single forty-watt bulb hung from a frayed cord midway down the shabby hallway. The light barely reached him, and he knew that he was virtually invisible, though exposed to anyone who might come out of one of the four apartments on the ground floor or down the staircase that ended near the front door.

After another fifteen-minute wait, he moved down the corridor to the stairwwell. He went up, taking two steps at a time, not to hasten his climb but to cut down on the number of squeaking treads. He'd heard nothing while waiting downstairs. Either the occupants of the building were sleeping, or the apartments were empty.

At the door to the front corner apartment, Carter listened. Still nothing, but warning bells began to jangle in his mind, and he had always heeded those bells.

Carter backtracked down the stairs and began jimmying locks on apartment doors. He checked all four apartments on the first floor. They were all empty. Was the whole building abandoned except for the one apartment on the second floor? he wondered.

He had to be sure. He opened all the apartments upstairs except the one in the front corner near the big wall and found three more empty apartments.

After making certain that there was no one lurking anywhere in the building, Carter returned to the corner apartment he had observed through the shutter. He approached the door with care. The fact that the rest of the building was deserted didn't guarantee that that apartment was empty. It could mean just the opposite. Raina and her friends could easily empty a building so no one would interrupt whatever little surprise that had planned.

Was the door a booby trap? Would someone start shooting at him through the wood when he tried to jimmy the lock or open the door? Or was there an automatic weapon attached to some clever device behind the door, and would it be triggered by his opening the door?

Carter stood aside and leaned over to work on the lock with Hugo's sharp point. He took a deep breath when he knew that the lock was about ready to pop.

The lock popped, but no bullets came at him through the door. He let out his breath and took another as he turned the knob.

Nothing happened.

Carter let the knob snap back into place and turned it to the left, again letting go. Then he carefully pushed open the door.

Carter waited, thoroughly familiar with delayed-action booby traps. He gave this one—if there was one—ten minutes, then tossed his jacket through the open doorway. To make certain, he snatched a big throw rug from the hall floor and waved it in the doorway. If an electronic triggering beam had been installed, the rug would do the job his body was supposed to do—and receive whatever had been arranged as a welcome.

Again nothing happened.

He peered around the corner into the apartment and saw the same living room he had seen from the outside. The lamp still burned on the small ornate table. The frayed furniture still sat alone and sedate, waiting for human occupancy. Carter slipped inside the room, and after making certain that no gunman lay waiting in the bedroom or kitchen, he propped the door open behind him.

"Welcome, Nick." Raina Missou's clear, sharp, sexy voice was as he remembered it. "I'm glad you made it through my little welcoming committee down the street. Come in, make yourself at home. My, my, it has been a long time since those pleasant interludes in my apartment in Casablanca, hasn't it."

In the pause, Carter looked around the room for the speakers. Raina's voice had been taped, and somehow he had triggered the message to begin.

"Isn't modern technology wonderful? I know exactly where you are, but you don't know where I am. If you have come this far, Nick," her honeyed voice oozed through the hidden, echoing speakers, "you might as well know where I really am. By the time the authorities discover your body in the building, everything will be academic. But I want you to know, darling, because you are going to die *by your own hand* in the next few minutes."

She had emphasized the words "by your own hand" so harshly that Carter felt like putting his hands into his pockets. He stopped in the middle of the room and gazed at the tables. The recorder, he was certain, was in a drawer of one of those tables. He waited through another pause.

"Still there, Nick?" Raina's voice asked. "Well, I hope so, because I wouldn't want you to miss this. I am in Paris now, and I'm with two other people you know quite

17

well. Remember Minya Stalin? Three years ago, you had a marvelous opportunity to kill him, but you let him go. Well, he's our leader, and he helped get me out of that atrocious jail. God, how I hate you for sending me there, just as I hate you for killing my father. And another of your old friends is with me in Paris. Remember Julio Vasco? He was a colonel in the Cuban marines when you last saw him on a mountainside in the Caribbean and did your best to kill him with that nasty little knife you carry. He's a general now and is also Minya Stalin's most trusted agent outside of Russia."

The tape hit another dead zone, and Carter found himself drawn to the little round table that held the lamp. He had noticed that there was a curved drawer in the side of the table. The recorder, he felt, had to be in there.

"I really don't know why I'm telling you all this, Nick," Raina's voice went on, bouncing off the walls of the stuffy little room. Carter realized why it was so close in there. Every window in the apartment was locked tightly in front of the closed outer shutters. Unusual. "But I guess I just can't let you die—by your own hand, remember—until you know just what's happening."

Carter was beside the table now. He could hear the clicking of parts as the reels of a small cassette tape recorder spun inside that drawer. He grinned, knowing that Raina Missou expected him to open that drawer. If he did, he was convinced that his action would trigger something. Something deadly. She'd hoped his curiosity would get the better of him, but again she underestimated him. He wouldn't open that drawer. Carter waited, his hands behind his back, as Raina's voice droned on.

"Remember my computer message in which I warned you and that nasty little man named Hawk that sophisticated equipment was being installed to tap into NATO's computers? Well, I knew that Hawk wouldn't believe we were *that* sophisticated, but we figured he'd send you anyway, just in case. We wanted you here in Tangier. Sooner or later, you'd get word of what we were doing and you'd come after us. It was Minya's idea to lure you into a trap and remove you as a threat before we proceeded with our plan."

Carter continued to stare at the table drawer. The recorder inside was whirring through the next pause.

"The plan," Raina explained, "is to fire a cruise missile at a section of barren desert in the southern part of Russia. That's all we need to do, just fire the missile. Whether it hits its target or not is immaterial. In fact, Minya is convinced that either your allies or the Russians will knock out that missile long before it reaches its target. The outcome of the firing is predictable. The Russians could but will not retaliate. What they will do is demand that the U.S. get all of its nuclear missiles out of Europe. What's more, the Europeans, who already have been demonstrating against the presence of missiles there, will be so much up in arms that you will have no choice but to remove them. And then Russia will have easy pickings to take over the balance of Europe and form one gigantic nation that the U.S. or its few remaining allies would never dare attack. How do you like the plan, Nick? If all goes well, the firing will be at dawn on Monday.

"Good-bye, Nick," Raina Missou said, her voice sounding a bit sad. "It was pleasant that time in Cassa-

19

blanca. But I'm running out of tape and I really have become bored with this monologue. Good-bye, Killmaster. You fought well, but you lost.''

The tape stopped and the drawer instantly popped open. Carter stared at the tape recorder and heard a distinct hissing sound in the heating ducts.

He couldn't smell anything, but you couldn't smell the gas Pierre contained, either. And that sound, to Carter's experienced ear, sounded just like a gas canister being released.

Instinctively, he slammed the drawer shut, hoping that his action would halt the issuance of lethal fumes.

Then he heard the little popping sound in the ventilator and knew what happened.

The hissing had been a lure, a ruse. The real triggering device of the deadly gas bomb in the heating ducts was the slamming of the table drawer, not the opening of it.

You are going to die by your own hand in the next few minutes.

Carter took a deep breath and ran for the open doorway, already feeling the stinging pain as the gas penetrated his eyes and nostrils. Now he realized why all the windows were shut tight. Raina had hoped the fumes would disperse rapidly enough to cause the room to become an instant gas chamber. But she hadn't counted on Carter's realizing so quickly what was happening and his immediate reaction.

He threw himself down the stairs, racing for the ground floor and the street.

THREE

Nick Carter lay panting on the street, breathing great gulps of the clear, early morning air. His throat and lungs felt as if they were on fire, and his eyes were awash with tears. His eyeballs and the inside of his mouth burned as if bathed with acid. His stomach was heaving, and he was drenched with icy sweat.

Hurtling down the stairwell seconds before, he realized that gas was being pumped into it as well as the apartment. He tried to keep his brain working, but the pain from the gas his body had already absorbed was so intense, he knew he didn't have much time left. At the bottom of the stairs he got his bearings, then plunged headfirst through the glass front door of the building, the sound of shattering glass like an explosion in the still darkness. He'd rolled down a short flight of cement steps and fell into the street.

When he felt he could make it, and could once again

breathe and see, he got to his feet and started to jog slowly away from 991 rue Vicenza.

Carter saw the red lights and police still at the scene where the original ambush had occurred, and he ducked into a side alley and lost himself in the labyrinth that was the Casbah.

He moved on, keeping to a downhill course, fighting back the pain and the nausea, and saw that the sky was beginning to lighten. Dawn was finally announcing the day ahead. He thought of Raina Missou's message to him on the tape.

If all goes well, the firing will be at dawn on Monday.

It was nearly dawn on Saturday, which gave the man from AXE just a hair over forty-eight hours to find Raina and the others, and to put a stop to their unthinkable plan.

They were in Paris, but where in Paris? It was a big city that Nick Carter knew well, but nobody knew it well enough to find three people and a staff of computer experts in forty-eight hours if they didn't want to be found.

The pain eased up some as Carter neared the bottom of the hill and the business section of the city. His plan was to get back to his hotel room and call Hawk in Washington. In this age of computers, it would be ridiculous not to put the best computers in the U.S. to work on the problem. And AXE's equipment was state of the art.

Carter could hear Hawk puffing on a cigar as he related the events of the past few hours.

"You made your way through sixteen men with automatic rifles?" Hawk chuckled. "Our boys in AXE field training must be doing something right."

22

But Carter knew that beneath Hawk's light words was concern for his premier agent and relief that he was all right. He had the mental image of his boss in his huge bed, enjoying his last terrible cigar of the day. It was 5:00 A.M. in Tangier which made it 11:00 P.M. in Washington, D.C.

"I don't understand it, sir. It seems that they *expected* me to survive that ambush. Otherwise, why go to all the trouble of emptying that building and rigging up that apartment with the tape and gas? Those men could have wasted me on that street if they'd really wanted to. And someone could have finished me off when I came flying out of that gas-filled apartment. They're creating these elaborate measures to kill me—and so far I'm still here. These people are not stupid or inept—and I'm fast, but I'm not superman. Their methods don't make any sense."

"I see your point," Hawk said, wheezing as he huffed out a great accumulation of smoke. "Why use the gas if they didn't think you'd be dropping by that apartment?"

"Raina really didn't give me anything to go on," Carter continued. "She said that she was telling me everything because she was certain I wouldn't make it out of there alive. And I almost didn't. All I know is that she, Stalin, and Vasco are in Paris. Or they were when she made the tape."

"Don't forget the part about sending a cruise missile to a remote target in the Soviet Union."

"I'm not," Carter replied, "but we don't know the target, except that it won't be a populated area. I'm not certain that Stalin is acting on orders from the top this time. I have the feeling that he's doing something to put himself in the good graces of his superiors. Since I sent him hightailing it home after he bungled my murder, I imagine he's been up to his neck in trouble—and bootlicking.''

Carter quickly thought of his last dealings with Minya Stalin three years before. Carter had made a deal with the crafty KGB agent so he could escape from a Russian trap. Even though Stalin had later tried to double-cross Carter and attempted to kill him, he was called on the carpet for what his superiors deemed to be treasonous acts. Carter wondered if Stalin had been imprisoned or sent to a camp in Siberia so he could have a chance to rethink and atone for his actions toward Carter. Carter was surprised that Stalin was out of the Soviet Union with Raina. Was he still with the KGB? Maybe the KGB thought he was too good an agent—or he knew too much—to kick out. He'd been punished, and maybe he still had one toe in the doghouse, but he was still part of the in crowd at Dzerzhinsky Square in Moscow. And he undoubtedly hated Carter's guts more than ever.

''If Minya Stalin can pull this off,'' Carter said, ''he'll be in solid with the KGB hierarchy. The Russians will get one of their greatest wishes: the pullout of all nuclear missiles from Western Europe. And Stalin's smart enough to know that now even the meanest bastard in the Kremlin would sacrifice a Soviet city to get rid of NATO's missiles. Or at least he wouldn't admit to such a sacrifice. By lobbying a fifty-kiloton nuclear missile into a Soviet desert, Stalin will achieve their purpose.'' Fifty kilotons, both men knew, constituted a formidable bomb. The one dropped on Hiroshima, for example, was only six and a half kilotons.

"So much for tonight's lesson in KGB logic," Hawk said. "Where does all this lead us?"

"First off, to Paris," Carter said. "But I have a feeling that's just another link in a long chain. God knows where they have the equipment that can hook into NATO's firing computers."

"*If* they have such equipment," Hawk added dubiously.

"I believe they have it," Carter admitted. "Anyway, sir, we have to proceed on the basis that they do. If they don't, we're home free if I can survive the ambushes they must have planned for me. This could be pure revenge, or it could be, as Raina Missou said, their way of getting rid of me before I picked up their trail in the ordinary day-to-day working with intelligence sources. It's hard to keep something like this a secret."

"If they'll be ready to send off one of our own damned missiles in forty-eight hours," Hawk snapped, "I'd say they've accomplished a hell of a lot in secret."

It was hard for both men to admit that their intelligence-gathering network had not come up with this potentially disastrous piece of information. The consequences for the Western powers were mind-boggling. Even Raina Missou's escape from prison was not routinely reported to Hawk and Carter. Was this an oversight on the part of Operations—or hadn't they known? AXE's eyes and ears were supposed to be everywhere, learning everything. Somebody somewhere had screwed up, Carter thought to himself.

It was obvious to Hawk and Carter, without it being mentioned, that work had commenced on the assembly of the computers long before Raina Missou was sprung from jail. Minya Stalin, the sharp KGB agent, had kept her out of it until the very end, knowing that an early jailbreak would have tipped off the West and hampered his plans to set up the ultrasophisticated equipment.

"Have you checked with the people at the prison where Missou was being kept?" Hawk asked, by way of covering all the bases. He assumed that Carter had checked with the prison before he had left for Tangier.

"Did that first thing," Carter replied. "Nothing unusual about it. Visitors brought in pieces of weapons for six people, including Raina. All six tried to escape to a van waiting on a side road, but only Raina and two others made it alive. There was nothing about it to suggest that Raina was the primary objective."

"And no sign of KGB involvement?"

"No. It looked more like a mob operation, as though the six had come up with a bundle of cash and bought a package escape deal. It's quite the new thing in Europe—package escape deals from the mob. The contact is made through an ordinary travel agency."

"Makes sense. They truly have the need to get away from it all," Hawk said wryly. "Anything else, N3?"

"I have nothing more to report, sir," a weary Nick Carter told his boss. "If you have no further questions, I think I'll grab a couple of hours of sleep, then head for Paris."

Hawk sighed. "Take care of yourself, Nick. Get some sleep and contact me when you get to Paris."

The Air France jet wobbled slightly in the crosswind

turbulence, then settled into its approach pattern like a robot suddenly hooked up to a ski-lift cable. The landing system in the aircraft anticipated the wind and turbulence, and corrected within a fraction of a second after it struck. The result was that the plane cut through the turbulence like a chainsaw through a log.

Nick Carter, asleep in his seat in the tourist section, was unaware of the windy conditions outside, and of the rain and sleet that lashed across the window inches away from his head.

Below, Orly Airport was awash with wind, rain, and sleet as the first big storm of winter moved across Europe from the already icy North Sea.

"*Monsieur*, we have arrived," the stewardess said softly to the sleeping man in the window seat. "Please return your seat to the upright position and fasten your safety belt."

Carter went through the movements automatically as he observed the marvelous sway of the woman's hips as she went on down the aisle to carry her pleasant message to other dozing passengers. Carter had every right to be sleepy. He hadn't caught that nap back in Tangier. Concern over the tight timetable and the fact that he could get a plane to Amsterdam within the hour altered his plans. From Amsterdam he had flown to Berlin, then to the tiny grand duchy of Luxembourg.

The roundabout route had cost him precious hours, but he figured it might end up saving his neck. If the triumvirate of assassins who had gathered to kill him before they placed the world on the brink of nuclear holocaust had set up another ambush at one of the two international airports in Paris, they would least expect him to be coming from Luxembourg.

There was no violent welcoming committee for him at Orly. He maintained high alert, though, even when he was outside in the howling storm trying to get a taxi. It had been cool in Tangier, but at least it had been calm—weatherwise, that is. Carter wore an all-weather trench coat, but the lining was packed in his suitcase, and he was shivering as he waited for the taxis to move along the curb, picking up passengers in order.

Before leaving Tangier, Carter had considered a number of options as to where to stay and under what name. He had briefly considered going to the lovely town house of Giselle Mondieux, a French businesswoman he had met some time ago, but he discarded that. He saw Giselle only between missions, not wanting to involve her in his usually violent activities. She was charming, pretty, intelligent, and just gullible enough to believe that he was a billionaire's bodyguard. How else was he to explain the weaponry he carried, on or off missions? After deciding not to involve Giselle, Carter had made several hotel reservations under his own name.

His turn for a taxi finally arrived, and he climbed into the rear seat, slammed the door, and cursed under his breath. The heater in the taxi wasn't turned on. The driver, a cigarette dangling from his lips, had his window all the way down. The icy rain was blowing into the cab, but the cabbie seemed oblivious to the weather, and to the fact that he had a wet, cold passenger.

"Are you an Eskimo, *monsieur*?" Carter asked in perfect French.

"*Pardon?*" the driver said.

"Please roll up your window and turn on the heater," Carter asked politely through chattering teeth. He didn't need this. Not now. He had visions of surviving Raina Missou and succumbing to pneumonia.

The Frenchman looked at him in the rearview mirror, shrugged, and rolled up the window and snapped on the heater.

Carter asked to be taken to the George V, one of the city's finest hotels. By the time the cab was on the highway going north toward Paris, he was warm and thinking about his situation. He wondered if Raina and her crew had anyone watching the airport and if he'd made it undetected so far.

He tipped the driver the bare minimum, then followed the uniformed bellman who carried his suitcase into the luxury hotel. He decided he deserved a little comfort after his recent escapades, and was glad he had decided on the deluxe George V.

He let his eyes roam around the opulent lobby, but he didn't spot a familiar or suspicious-looking face. No one was waiting for him except the reservations clerk at the front desk.

"Ah, Monsieur Carter," the man said. "Here is your reservation. If you would be so kind as to fill out this card, I will have a bellman take you to your room."

Carter signed the registration form and tipped lavishly all the way up to his suite, then crashed on the bed and slept like the dead.

Downstairs, a greasy-haired little man in a tan suit went to a public telephone.

"This is Squeeze at the George Cinq," the man said in

English. "Your guy just showed. He don't look so tough to me."

"Thank you," a female voice responded. "Don't let appearances deceive you. And stay where you are. Call this number again when he leaves the hotel."

"Sure thing, babe."

"Call me 'babe' once more, Mr. Squeeze," Raina Missou told the little man with the Brooklyn accent, "and you will become part of the garbage that floats on the Seine. Good-bye."

FOUR

Several hours later, Nick Carter, much refreshed after a nap, a shower and shave, a change of clothes, and a meal delivered to his room with a cold beer, stepped from the elevator that looked like an ornate birdcage. On his way through the lobby to drop off his room key, he saw the man with the greasy hair and wondered if he had been there when he'd arrived. Carter didn't remember seeing him when he'd cased the lobby before registering.

Even though he knew that the little man, who sat in a plush chair and pretended to read a copy of *Paris Match*, was watching with beady black eyes as he went about his departure from the hotel, the Killmaster played the game to the hilt. Carter scanned the lobby a few times, and was amused when the man tried to become invisible under his gaze. He even caught the watcher's eyes and held them for a moment. A smile touched the corners of his lips, as if to say, "I see you now, but what are you going to do about it?"

Carter was thankful for the presence of the little man. He might be of some help to him. Hawk had run every possible question through AXE's computers but had come up with nothing. There was no indication that anyone was setting up special computer hardware in Paris, either as part of legitimate business or clandestinely.

Carter had arrived in Paris with absolutely no leads, no ideas of where to proceed. He had come to Paris only because Raina had mentioned it and because he had no other place to start his search.

He had come to Paris as bait.

If he could not find the three who wanted him dead and who would put the world in nuclear jeopardy, he would let *them* find *him*.

Raina must have been surprised that Carter's body was not discovered in that second-floor apartment of that run-down building in the Casbah. She would make certain that her third try on his life would be impossible for him to survive. He would have to watch every step he took in Paris very carefully.

And Nick Carter knew that he had to face whatever she and her partners would set up—and survive it—or the world would be in deep trouble very soon.

Even Hawk had agreed that the Russians would not wait for an inquiry if a cruise missile were fired from a European base at any spot in the U.S.S.R.

The Russians would destroy the weapon if they could, then retaliate with a hail of missiles and ask questions later—if there was a later.

Carter made certain that the man with the greasy hair knew he'd been spotted. If the little man knew that Carter knew, things might get interesting.

But the ferretlike man didn't follow Carter outside. Carter hailed a taxi and got in slowly, watching the hotel's entrance and hoping the man would at least come outside. Perhaps the man would ask the doorman if he knew Carter's destination. Would he be that brazen about his surveillance of Carter?

Carter sat inside the taxi, still watching the doorway. The little man did not emerge. He asked the taxi driver to wait a few moments, explaining that he was expecting someone who was now in the lobby to join him. After a minute or two, Carter apologized to the driver and mumbled something about how his friend must be having some problem checking out. He gave the cabbie a few francs for his time, then got out of the cab and returned to the hotel lobby.

Inside, Carter's eyes flitted quickly to the bank of telephones opposite the main desk near the entrance to the elegant dining room. The man with the greasy hair was using one of the phones, and he looked panic-stricken when he saw the tall, well-built, dark-haired man he'd been paid to watch march straight toward him with heavy, purposeful, angry strides.

"My God, he's made me!" he said into the phone. "He's coming toward me! Christ . . ."

Squeeze dropped the receiver and let it dangle, clanking against the wall below. He got two strides away from the telephone before Nick Carter grabbed him by the shoulder and pressed him to the wall. The man tried to get away, but Carter had him pinned. As if nothing unusual were happening—it wouldn't be polite to cause a scene in the lobby of the George V—Carter calmly retrieved the receiver and put it to his ear.

"Hello? Hello?" Raina's usually well-modulated voice was impatient. "Squeeze, are you there? What is happening?"

"Oh, not much, Raina," Carter said casually. "What's happening with you?"

"Nick!" It was a strange sound to the man who had heard variations of it all his life. It wasn't really his name that Raina Missou had shot back through the phone line. It was part grunt, part obscenity, and part exclamation of shock and surprise.

"The one and only," Carter said lightly. "Are you here in Paris, or did Squeeze have to make a long distance call?"

Raina, who had obviously lost her composure at the sound of his voice, quickly regained it.

"You haven't changed, Nick," she said smoothly. "I suppose my man ran out on us."

"Ran like a headless chicken," Carter lied. Carter now had his hand around the base of Squeeze's throat, holding him to the wall beside the phone. The man had given up any attempt at escape, surrendering to Carter's superior size and strength. "What was he telling you, Raina? That I was leaving the hotel? Now you tell me: What's waiting for me out there?"

Raina's laugh was musical, just as he remembered it. It conjured up nights in her Casablanca apartment a long time ago.

"You'll find out soon enough, Nick," she said. "My, but it took you long enough to get here. Do you realize that in less than forty hours, we will live up to my promise to you?"

"That's a lot of time," Carter said, trying to keep her on the line. If this were a local call, the prepaid time would run out shortly on the pay telephone, and the operator would cut in. If it were long distance, a three-minute warning might be given, and Carter would know where Raina was by the language the operator used, or by her accent. "By the way, Raina, I—"

"Good-bye, Nick. I won't stay on the line and let you learn where I am—or where I am not. One hint, though. You might find what you seek at the Septien Club, say in two hours."

The click stopped any response that Carter might have made. He knew the Septien Club, or knew where it was. It was a dismal section of Paris where the crime rate had soared in the past ten years.

A gagging sound and an ache in his shoulder reminded Carter that he was still holding Raina's employee at arm's length, jammed up against the wall, his fingers tight on the man's skinny neck. He lowered the man, got a grip on his arm, and then took him outside where the cold might loosen a tight tongue. The two men walked, almost in lockstep, for about ten minutes until they found a narrow, deserted passageway between two buildings. Carter shoved him into the little alley and slammed him up against a brick wall.

"All right, Squeeze, start talking," he ordered. "Tell me all you know. If I think you're holding back one piece of information, you'll wish you'd never seen my face.''

An hour later, Nick Carter was convinced that Raina was indeed in Paris, because Squeeze had been hired to call a Paris number, but the man from Brooklyn knew nothing else of value. He was a low-level mob courier, imported because he was owed a favor, and he was instructed to keep an eye out for a man answering Carter's description. He had been in Paris for only two days.

Squeeze was leveling, Carter knew. He let go of his arm, and the little man took off as fast as his legs could carry him.

Now Carter had some time to kill. He had no intention of turning up at the Septien Club at the suggested time, which would be in about another hour. If the assassins had gathered for him there, they would have to wait. Carter walked back to the George V and hailed another taxi.

"Where would you wish to go on this miserably cold but otherwise marvelous Saturday night in Paris, *monsieur?*" the smiling cabbie asked.

"Just drive down the Champs-Élysées," Carter said within earshot of the doorman. "I want to sightsee." A block away he gave the cabbie Giselle Mondieux's address.

Giselle was the antithesis of Raina Missou in many ways. Where Raina was golden-skinned, dark-haired, and openly sensual, Giselle was pale, blonde, and almost prim, her slim body encased in expensive, impeccably tailored suits and dresses. Giselle was a successful businesswoman who ran a small, exclusive porcelain shop on a fashionable street on the Right Bank.

The lovely Frenchwoman with the ivory complexion

and aristocratic features lived on the fashionable Avenue St. Cloud near the Bois de Boulougne. The town house was easily in the half-million-dollar range. Everything about her said luxury and taste and good breeding. As the taxi rumbled along around the Arc de Triomphe and down Avenue Foch toward Paris's largest and most beautiful park, Nick Carter relaxed and remembered his moments with Giselle Mondieux.

He had met her when he was on vacation, between missions. She was sad and lonely then, and heartbroken. Her business partner and lover of many years had died some months before, and Giselle was running the business by herself. Carter, caught by the beautiful vases and platters in the window—and by the lovely woman he saw behind the counter—decided to step in and buy a gift or two. Carter wound up taking the shop's owner to dinner, and, eventually, to bed. And much to his surprise and delight, once the suit was hung in the closet and the neat, twisted hairdo was brushed loose, she became a tigress.

In the ensuing years, Carter had made it a point to avoid Giselle when he was in Paris on a mission. He never wanted her to become entangled in his work. It was too dangerous. He'd never forgive himself if something happened to her because some international thug supposed that she was part of Carter's team. But right now, he wanted some calm before the storm. He needed to be with a good person who was not part of his crazy life.

Giselle was just that soothing port in the storm.

"Oh, Nicholas, *mon cher*, why did you not tell me you were coming? I look a mess . . ."

Giselle Mondieux looked anything but a mess to Nick Carter as he stood in the doorway of her home and felt the warmth of the interior rush out to meet him. She wore a dirty smock because she had a workshop and kiln on the ground floor, and created some of the ceramics sold in the shop. She was a true artist, and as any potter would be, caught in the excitement of creation, she was covered in clay to the elbows.

Carter cocked his head and looked at her appraisingly. "I do think a bath is in order before we put you on the cover of *Vogue*."

She laughed and motioned him to come inside so she could close the heavy, ornate front door against the cold. Carter took her face in his hands and gave her a quick kiss.

"When did you arrive in Paris?" she asked him, wiping her hands and arms on her smock. "How long can you stay? I will close the shop Monday and Tuesday and Wednesday and . . . and we shall have a wonderful time together."

"I'm sorry, Giselle," he said. "This time I'm here on a business trip, and I have only a little time to spare—two hours at most."

Giselle stood back and regarded the tall, handsome man who was so welcome in her house and in her life.

"You cannot be serious."

"I wish I weren't. Can I have a drink? It's awfully cold out there, and just the sight of you is like a warm bath, but my insides need warming up, too."

"Of course, Nicholas. Come into the living room and explain to me why it is that you have come to me for only two hours. That is not fair, you know. You arrive—and then you have to go."

While she poured two snifters of cognac, Carter told her that his employer was closing an important business deal in Europe, but he couldn't afford to be away for very long from his affairs in the States. Thinking fast, Carter explained how his boss, a platoon of lawyers and aides, and, of course, Carter had boarded that morning's Concorde in New York. After the negotiations were done and the papers signed, a chartered jet was ready and waiting to take them back to New York immediately. Once Carter had seen his charge safely to the offices where all this high finance was taking place, he'd been dismissed and told to amuse himself for a few hours.

And that's how he came to be on her doorstep unannounced and on a tight schedule.

"I can't tell you what the business is, because I don't know myself, but I can tell you one thing," Carter said, tilting her face to his and looking into the large hazel eyes above the wide, sensual mouth, "I've missed you and I'll treasure even the small amount of time we will have together."

"That is two things," Giselle corrected, "but you are forgiven. A brief visit is better than none."

She took his face in her hands and pulled it down so that their lips met. Her tongue slid slowly along Carter's lips, teasing them apart.

"I think I will take that bath you suggested," she murmured. "Why don't you wait for me upstairs?"

Carter followed her up the elegant curved staircase that led to the upper floors and her bedroom.

When she emerged from the adjoining bathroom, she walked directly to Carter, who lay on the bed sipping his drink. He'd refilled the snifters, and her glass rested on the little table beside the bed.

He reached up and pulled the sash from the raspberry-colored robe. Carter admired the incredible slimness of her body, the fine bones wrapped in silken flesh. He pulled her to him, feeling the taut stomach muscles press against his. Her blond head, the hair cascading over them both, nuzzled into the hollow of his neck, her teeth nipping at his shoulder.

Giselle moaned as she felt his hands on her body, then her mouth was on his chest, the moisture of her tongue and lips leaving a path of heat along the side of his rib cage. Her fingers traced lazy circles along the length of his thighs, stroking, fondling, touching. Carter's hand gently pressed her downward onto him, the shape of her delicate head impressing itself into his palm.

When he could bear her mouth no longer, he reached down with both arms and in one strong motion pulled her up and rolled her exquisite body beneath him. Her legs parted and wrapped themselves around his waist.

When they finally moved together, locked in sexual embrace on the canopied bed in her antique-filled bedroom, all traces of worry vanished from Carter's mind. At that moment in time he could forget that he was an agent for one of the world's most secret espionage organizations. He was the lover of a beautiful woman.

Giselle, in turn, was no longer just a sharp business-woman or an artist. She was a sensual creature of passionate desires and deep hungers. Nick Carter was one of the few men in her life who had discovered all the special places on her body that gave her the most intense pleasure. If she thought she could have him all to herself, she would hire him away from the inconsiderate billionaire, but she knew that men like Carter were like precious gems. They were made to be enjoyed, but the owner would always live in fear of losing the treasure, so could never completely relax with that prize possession.

But just then she was in possession of this extraordinary man, and she clutched at his back, cried out, and twisted against him, wanting to somehow make it last forever and ever, for him and for her, and wanting, at the same time, the final inevitable explosion that would make them one, just for that moment.

FIVE

The Septien Club was not the garish display of neon and girlie photos that Nick Carter had expected. It was a dark place, a converted town house once owned and lived in by a wealthy Parisian of the last century, later a bordello, and then an apartment building for hungry artists. Now the upstairs rooms were empty and dark; all the action was in the huge cellar where wine racks once held the finest French champagnes.

Carter had left Giselle's house thirty minutes ago. They had talked, sipped cognac, cursed Carter's boss for his frantic schedule, and had made love again. He had walked from her house, knowing that she was watching, and waited on the street corner for a taxi.

Carter had left the taxi on a wide avenue and, hands deep in his pockets and shoulders hunched against the cold, walked through the tough neighborhood where both artists and whores displayed their wares. Carter had approached the Septien Club, which sat on a small side street that led downhill at a steep angle, with utmost caution. He would move from one doorway to another, then cross the street, then cross back again. His keen eyes scanned windows and roofs.

By the time he had come to the street on which the club was located, he had the neighborhood and its buildings etched in his memory like a drawing on a draftsman's table.

As he had done in Tangier, he took to the roofs and, finding them clear, worked his way slowly across buildings until he was directly on top of the roof of the Septien Club with its many dormers and chimneys.

Carter could feel the throb of music from the small band through the timbers of the old house. He found an unlocked window in a gable, slipped inside a dark room, and listened. He could hear the music from the basement, and even an occasional laugh from a sharp-voiced woman patron. A female vocalist was imitating the husky, throaty voice and style of Marlene Dietrich.

Slowly, picking his way through the darkness of the big empty house, Nick Carter made his way to the second floor, then to the first. He opened a door at the bottom of the stairwell and saw a long, dimly lighted corridor. At the rear of the house, a solid steel door reflected the light from the front. Carter scanned the corridor, looking for movement around the occasional dark shape of a piece of furniture. His eyes finally reached the front door where a desk was set up. Seated there were two powerful-looking bouncers. The doors leading to the street were of plate glass.

THE ASSASSIN CONVENTION

As Carter watched, one of the doors opened and a laughing couple came in on a gust of north wind. Carter shivered. He was still cold from his long, slow trek over the roofs. The newly arrived couple paid the two goons at the table and were admitted to another door off the side of the corridor. When that door was opened, sounds of revelry and music and the phony Marlene Dietrich burst out and filled the corridor. When the door was closed again, the sounds were muted.

Carter decided that it wouldn't be smart to face those tough-looking bruisers who guarded the door and sold tickets to the Septien Club. He closed the door and flicked his lighter, which gave him just enough light to check out the stair landing.

There was a smaller door at the end of a narrow secondary hallway. He went to it and found it locked. He figured it was probably the employees' entrance, and each employee had a key. Carter had no key, but he had his stiletto. In twenty seconds he had the door opened and smelled the aromas of food surging up from below. He was directly above the kitchen.

Going down, he palmed his Luger just in case. If Raina Missou had arranged another ambush, she would have warned her hired gunmen to keep a wary eye out for the unexpected. Carter was surprised that this entry to the Septien Club hadn't been blocked by a whole gaggle of gunmen strewn along the way like mines in a field. Either they were looking for him to come in the front way, they weren't looking for him at all, or, and Carter suspected this was the case, they *wanted* him to get inside the club the back way.

If this last possibility were true, he could expect Raina Missou and Company to pull out all the stops to nail his hide to the wall. What awaited him in the basement could easily make what had awaited him in Tangier seem tame by comparison.

At the bottom of the rear staircase, he had several options. The door to the kitchen stood open, and he could see chefs and helpers and busboys and waiters dashing around in the confined space, yelling to one another. Considering what looked to be complete chaos, Carter was amazed that food could be ordered, cooked, and served to the correct customer. The kitchen was bedlam.

Two other doors led off the small hallway. Both were closed. Carter guessed that the door marked Private was the manager's office. But the second? It could lead to another staircase, a bedroom, a wine cellar, or even directly into the main room of the club.

The door did lead into the dining room, and Carter chose to enter the dark private office instead of the club. He searched the walls until he found what he was seeking: a large painting that covered a one-way mirror. He could see into the dining room, but the people inside saw nothing but themselves in the mirrored surface of the window's opposite side.

And there, right at ringside, gazing up at the phony Marlene Dietrich and listening to her new song of woe, was Raina Missou. She was sitting alone at a small table, but Carter made out at least a half-dozen armed men sitting at tables in a semicircle around the still beautiful woman.

It occurred to Carter, as he watched the lovely woman

who had once tried her best to kill him and almost succeeded, that he could easily kill her right then and there. He could fire one shot from Wilhelmina, letting the 9mm hunk of hot lead shatter the one-way mirror on its way to that beautiful head. But killing her would not end the threat; it would bring the thugs streaking toward him like a swarm of angry hornets. He couldn't take them all out with the Luger and the stiletto, and to use Pierre in this crowded place would be cruel as well as suicidal.

Carter holstered the Luger and watched Raina, remembering those Casablanca nights and the softness of her skin and the ardor of her lovemaking. He also remembered that terrible moment when he watched Raina Missou slowly pull the trigger on a pistol she had hidden between her ample breasts.

Carter sighed, thinking of both the good and the bad. And now, he wondered, what would happen next? What did Raina Missou have in mind, luring him to this dark club in the sleaziest part of Montmartre, then sitting calm and composed at the edge of the little stage listening to a poor imitation of Marlene Dietrich?

"Do you like what you see, Nick Carter?" Raina Missou's voice boomed in the dark office. Startled, he whirled around toward the voice. And then he realized that he was watching its owner through the glass and that the words, as they had been in that deathtrap in Tangier, were on tape.

Carter remained silent, fearful that the tape recorder might be rigged to trigger a bobby trap if an alien voice reached its sensitive electronic apparatus. But he dropped to the floor, his arm outstretched toward the sound of the voice, his Luger gripped tightly in his hand.

"I knew you would come," Raina's recorded voice continued. "And I knew you would find this room. You are so predictable, Nick. Did you enjoy your climb over the roofs of Montmartre? I have a small beeper that told me when you entered the manager's office. It cost only a few American dollars to set up this new welcome for you. Good-bye, Nick Carter."

Carter's first instinct was to run for the door. He expected gas, then discarded that. Raina knew that poison gas would seep into the nightclub, endangering herself, which she would never risk. His mind considered a bomb, and for the same reason he had discarded poison, he discarded a bomb. Any device powerful enough to kill him would blow out the one-way mirror and send shards of glass into the crowd, possibly right into the beautiful face of Raina Missou.

And then he guessed. Raina expected him to make a run for the office door. Somehow she had rigged the office to concentrate firepower on that door. His eyes searched the dark room, and he picked out the pinpoints of light that indicated a beam activator. Once he broke that beam a second time, all hell would break loose in the form of a hail of bullets from every conceivable direction. Even if the rigged weapons in the dark office walls and ceiling missed him, the initial shots would send Raina Missou's hired thugs racing into the hallway outside to pump him full of lead.

And so he did the unexpected one more time.

Nick Carter backed up to the manager's desk. With Wilhelmina in one hand and Hugo in the other, he raced across the room and plunged headlong through the one-way mirror.

He had calculated his landing so he'd fall on his back on an empty table just below the mirror. He would flip completely over and come up on his feet, just a few yards away from Raina and her bodyguards. He would kill her first, then take out as many thugs as possible. But he didn't think that would be necessary. He had considered one other possibility.

And it happened.

As soon as the glass exploded, Raina Missou took a header from her chair and scurried away on her hands and knees.

When Nick Carter's twisting body hit the table, Raina Missou was already out of sight. When Carter pushed himself to his feet, he was gazing at the astonished faces of hired thugs who hadn't counted on this kind of a difficulty factor.

Raina Missou had no doubt assured them that they were here only as a backup, just in case, and here they found themselves face to face with a madman who crashed through a mirror into a crowded nightclub.

The place was a melee of screaming patrons. Carter, still crouched in the kill position, decided to hold his fire. *Let them go*. He knew that Raina was crawling through the hysterical crowd. *Let her go, too*.

He ran to the door that led back to the small corridor outside the kitchen and went swiftly up the stairs. He retraced his steps all the way to the roof and ran quickly but carefully to the front of the building. He was looking down on the steep street. Already, people were pouring out of the Septien Club, afraid the lunatic with the knife and the gun might come crashing through the front doors after them.

A black Mercedes was moving up the narrow street. Carter wondered if it were Raina's. He waited.

Sure enough, the car eased to the curb, and the chauffeur got out and opened the curbside rear door. Raina Missou, looking pale and frightened, dashed across the sidewalk.

Nick Carter was so busy watching the woman get into the car, he didn't see the man who had detached himself from the crowd and was across the street.

The man opened fire with a .45 automatic.

The heavy slugs pounded into the roof, inches away from Carter's face.

And then he felt the hammerblow as a bullet struck him on the upper right side of his head.

He had the sensation of floating, then he felt shooting pains in both arms. He wasn't floating, he was rolling. Over and over on the steep roof, heading for the ground.

Carter remembered putting out his hands and feeling them get slapped by cold, rough roofing tiles. He remembered that his body stopped rolling suddenly and that something hard slammed into his ribs, knocking the breath out of his lungs.

And then he was floating again and then he was not floating and then he was no longer in pain and no longer in fear and no longer aware of the cold.

If this is death, he thought as the feeling of total numbness continued to absorb him, *it isn't so bad*.

He awoke slowly, even though his entire body was shivering so hard that the roof was creaking. The skies were an open wound of wet and cold above him, and he heard the clatter of sleet all around him. He was shivering from a cold that he had never known could be so all-consuming.

There were aches throughout his body, but one was special. It was near the top of his head, on the right side. He reached up and touched it. From the dim glow of a nearby streetlight, he saw blood on his fingers. His own blood. Was it fresh, or was the rain keeping it wet? He checked his watch and groaned.

He had been lying unconscious in the crotch of the roof for almost four hours.

He remembered the man from across the street and the big, booming .45. He remembered seeing Raina make her escape in the black Mercedes. He remembered the sound of the heavy slugs and the sight of flying debris from the edge of the roof.

And he remembered the moment when one lucky shot caught him on the head and he rolled and floated and rolled and slammed into something hard. He had thought he was dead.

Slowly, painfully, Carter worked himself out of the vee of the roof, nodded his thanks to the nineteenth-century architect who had designed a roof that would one day save a man's life, and crawled back the way he had come. An hour later, much colder but feeling a little steadier, he found a late-cruising taxi.

He gave the taxi driver Giselle Mondieux's address and sat back in the plastic-covered seat to rest and, hopefully, to gain strength. The bullet had just grazed his head, causing more bleeding than actual damage. If he could clean the wound, get a drink, and get some sleep, he knew he'd be all right.

His mind tried to recall the events of the evening to

ferret out the mistake that had put him in this position, but his abused body refused to let his mind do any more work. He shut off all thought and closed his eyes, riding along in a fog. He wasn't certain if he tipped the driver when he got out. He just gave the man a roll of francs and staggered into the night.

Giselle opened her front door on his fifth ring. He literally fell into her arms.

"Nicholas! *Mon Dieu!*" she cried, collapsing under his weight and letting her big, liquid eyes take in his bloody head and ripped clothes. "What happened to you?"

Carter looked at her face, opened his mouth to say something—just what he wasn't sure—then let the warmth of her house and the painlessness of oblivion enfold him.

"There will be no more attempts to stop this man," Minya Stalin said as he sat at the head of the table in the bright room. "We are needed at the lighthouse. There is no way that he can trace us there."

"Don't be too certain," Raina Missou replied. She spoke in a subdued voice, recalling the sight of Nick Carter as he came crashing through that mirror. She had counted on just about everything but that. In that moment, she had almost admired the man who had killed her father five years ago and sent her to prison. Almost, but not quite. "Wouldn't you agree, General Vasco, that Mr. Carter can never be counted out?"

Seated directly across the table from Raina was a man whose face revealed that he had done many brutal things in his fifty years of existence. He was tall and broad, with a wild thatch of yellowing white hair and a beard to match. These had been black, just giving in to gray, when Carter had first seen him on the island of Nicarxa. The hair and beard had turned white virtually overnight, after Carter had cut his throat and stabbed him in the chest. He had survived to do even crueler things than he had done before, and lived now with a zigzag scar across his thick neck. The scar on his chest was hidden by a khaki uniform bedecked with a colorful array of medals.

"The first time I saw this man," the general said, his voice deep and gravelly, as if he needed to clear his throat but decided not to, "I thought he was stupid. He was pretending to be one of my soldiers, a sergeant. He fooled me by playing stupid. When I finaly learned of his cleverness, it was too late." He emphasized his final remark by gingerly touching the long white scar just beneath his beard.

"But would you agree that we should eliminate him before we depart for the lighthouse and the final countdown to the firing?" Raina persisted.

"Indeed I would," General Vasco said.

They both looked at Minya Stalin at the head of the table. He had a plain, almost ordinary face, but there were qualities of intensity and intelligence and viciousness in the dead gray eyes. Stalin was a master of disguise and had tried to fool Carter many times in the past. The eyes always gave him away. Stalin was only of average height and build, but those eyes lent stature—he *seemed* huge.

"So that makes the vote two to one against me," Stalin said, smiling with only his mouth; his eyes locked with his companions' in silent combat. "If we were in America, or had been brainwashed by the CIA, I would consider myself defeated by this vote. But I must remind you that this is my plan and that we will be in Soviet territory when we reach the lighthouse. We cannot do this thing democratically, as they say, even if we felt so inclined. We leave at noon. That will give us plenty of time to type in the necessary codes, but we must allow extra time in case anything goes wrong. The last word from my people in Poland is that the equipment has been installed and is being tested. It should be perfect by the time we get there. So—we leave at noon.''

There was silence in the big room. They sat in a dining room in a very fine house. The town house, located not far from the one in which Giselle Mondieux lived, had been rented weeks ago by Minya Stalin as he slowly and carefully laid his plans for this great caper that would stand him in good stead with the military and political leaders of the Kremlin and Politburo.

Raina Missou, still eager to exact her pound of flesh from the seemingly invincible agent named Nick Carter, grudgingly nodded in agreement. She was almost certain that one of her men had killed Nick Carter on the roof of the Septien Club, but none of her hired thugs had had the nerve to go up and check. She had reported all this truthfully to Minya Stalin and General Vasco, and Stalin chose to believe that Carter had been killed. After all, he had been shot in the head when he was at the peak of a gable on the roof. The man who shot him had said that Carter had rolled wildly out of sight down the steep roof. Even if the bullet had not killed him, the fall to the street would have finished the job.

But there was one thing Raina Missou had not told her partners. As soon as she had arrived in Paris, she had contacted a certain female friend of Carter. Raina had learned of this woman during her five years in prison. Using outside contacts, she had learned many things about Nick Carter. The one impenetrable area had been the exact nature of Carter's employer. She learned that he worked for the U.S. government, but she could not learn the name or the purpose of his agency. Her spies had eliminated the FBI and the CIA as possibilities, and he was not a special emissary from the U.S. President. Whatever agency Carter worked for, Raina had assumed, was damned special and damned secret and damned powerful.

In her talk with the female friend, Raina had made it plain that it was important that she be told if Nick Carter showed up at her house, which she knew he did every so often. She explained that she was an old friend—an old lover, she admitted hesitantly—or a former boss of Nick Carter. To Raina, "former boss" sounded just vague enough to avoid any questions; most people worked for somebody at some point. She apologized for having spied on Carter the last time he'd been in Paris—how else would she have known the woman's address?—but she was desperate to send a message to her ex-boyfriend. She rambled on, and the woman seemed to be buying her story.

Raina had indeed been keeping tabs on Carter during her years in prison. Her father had stashed away millions of dollars in Swiss bank accounts before Carter had cornered and finally killed him. Through contacts, and with promises of repayment from those accounts once she got out—the accounts had been in both her father's and Raina's names—she had directed her people to keep track of Nick Carter and his friends. When she got out of jail, she would know exactly where he was.

Raina gave a convincing performance of being upset and preyed on the Frenchwoman's sympathetic feelings for another woman's distress in an affair of the heart. The woman was to call Raina the next time Carter visited her and tell of his plans if she knew what they were.

Her charade worked. The woman had called last evening to say that Carter had been at her house and had left to escort the American businessman for whom he now worked back to the States. To Raina, it sounded like one of Carter's crazy stories. She received word of the call at her table at the Septien Club and knew then that Carter was on the way to the club. She had only to wait.

And then the son of a bitch had fallen into her trap only to crash out of it.

No, Nick Carter was not dead on that roof. She saw no reason to send anyone to check. He was gone from there. If he had been hit, he would probably find his way to his female friend's house. She'd bet on it.

When the telephone at the far end of the table rang, Raina Missou nearly leaped out of her skin. She had been expecting a call, hoping for it, but the actual ringing had startled her from a favorite reverie—imagining the death of Nick Carter.

Minya Stalin got up slowly. It was almost dawn and he was exhausted. He answered the telephone, then held out the receiver to Raina.

"You have more people in the field than the KGB," he said. "This one's a woman."

"Hello? Raina? This is Giselle," the anxious voice came through the line. "Nick Carter has just come back to my house. He has been wounded somehow and is suffering from exposure . . . I do not know what happened . . . I do not know how to contact his employer . . . He has a head wound and has been unconscious—"

"Calm down, Giselle. Everything'll be all right. I'll come right over and help you. Keep him warm and pour yourself a brandy. I'm leaving now," Raina said, smiling triumphantly at the KGB man and the Cuban general. "I'll be there very soon. He'll be fine, whatever happened. I'll take care of everything," she added soothingly, then hung up.

"It is something I must do," Raina said to the two men, snatching her fur coat from the back of an empty chair. "I will meet you at Orly Airport at noon, and I will be able to report then that Nick Carter is indeed dead."

SIX

Nick Carter lay on the big canopied bed in the dark bedroom, his eyes closed, his mind occupied with a dizzying kaleidoscope of dreams that ranged from the wildly sexual to the desperately dangerous. His dreams were often an instant reply of recent events, and the previous twelve hours had indeed been busy.

There was no blood on his face or hair now, and the neat white bandage was the only evidence that a bullet had been anywhere near him. There were bruises on his face from the tumbling on the rough roof, and his hands looked as though he had worked a stint as a careless butcher. Otherwise, there was no indication that he had done anything the night before but sleep in his shorts in a very feminine bed.

Giselle Mondieux came into the room and stared at him for a time. She shook her head, recalling the few stories

Nick Carter had told her about his work, and then the stories she had just heard from that lovely Moroccan woman, Raina Missou.

Yes, it was possible that the stories were all intertwined. Carter had told her that he was a bodyguard for an eccentric American billionaire. Well, suppose only part of the story were true? Was Carter in truth a bodyguard for the dictator of the Third World country the charming, golden-skinned woman had mentioned? Wouldn't such a madman have international political ambitions? Couldn't Carter be a part of his crazy terrorist schemes? Why would Raina Missou tell her all this if it weren't true? After all, she hardly knew Carter . . . Not really. . . .

Was it possible that Nick Carter, in his role as protector for the dictator, had murdered Raina Missou's father and arranged to have her sent to prison for five years, even though both were innocent of any crimes? What had she said that she and her father had done? Oh, yes, they were at a meeting in Casablanca where the fanatical dictator was speaking. She and her father had dared to stand up and oppose some of the dictator's ideas and plans to absorb Morocco into his own country.

For this, Raina Missou had said, Nick Carter had been sent to kill her father and to arrange for the daughter's imprisonment in her own country. She had apologized to Giselle for making up the story about the old boyfriend, but she hoped Giselle would realize how important it was for her to see Carter again. Giselle was frightened by all this stunning information, but she had listened to every word.

And what had really happened last night? Carter had said that he had to get back to his employer, and returned wounded and half frozen. The cruel dictator had obviously learned that Raina Missou was out of prison and in Paris. He must have sent Carter to kill her, and the plan had somehow backfired.

Giselle stood in the doorway, watching the sleeping figure of the man who was such a mystery. She didn't want anything to happen to Nick Carter. She could understand Raina Missou's desire for revenge, and if she were telling the truth, she deserved revenge. If Nick Carter were protecting that madman who ruled that small but influential North African country, he deserved to be brought down.

It had not occurred to Giselle Mondieux that Raina Missou would go so far as to kill Nick Carter. The woman might employ men to take Carter out into the country and—what was it gangsters said in the movies?—work him over.

But murder certainly was not part of the picture, Giselle believed.

And yet even the thought of Nick Carter being beaten up made Giselle falter in her resolve. The man had obviously been through a great deal during the night. He needed rest and care, not another rough time.

Giselle Mondieux wrestled with her conscience, and thought of the beautiful woman seated in her living room. With a deep sigh and one final look back at the handsome face of the sleeping man, Giselle left the bedroom, put on her long mink coat, and went out the back door to the two-car garage. She chose the Ferrari because she wanted to drive fast and far on this stormy day.

She had agreed to Raina Missou's request that she leave the house, and Raina had promised that anything that happened to Nick Carter would never be traced to her or to this house.

Tears flowed down her cheeks as the Ferrari picked up speed, and Giselle Mondieux had the terrible feeling that she would never see the mysterious man named Nick Carter again. Not alive, anyway.

From the tall windows of the elegant salon, Raina Missou watched the sleek red sports car go out of the driveway. She saw the beautiful but sad-faced woman behind the wheel. Even through the driving rain and sleet, she knew that the woman was either crying or very close to it. She understood. As much as she hated Nick Carter, she had to acknowledge his power over women. Not even she had been immune from that.

But the man she knew only as some kind of government agent with considerable influence had proved too slippery for her again and again.

This time, though, he was out of commission. He was unconscious from a head wound and exposure. He was upstairs in the pretty bedroom of sweet, trusting Giselle Mondieux. Carter would be easy pickings for her this morning. At long last.

Nick Carter was dreaming that he was Gulliver and that the Lilliputians were crisscrossing his body with tiny strings, staking him to the ground. The little people from the imagination of Jonathan Swift were all over the man from AXE, tying down a finger here, an ear there, a hank of hair in another place. The busy little people had woven a virtual cocoon of rope around Carter, and he realized that he could not possibly break out on his own.

And then Carter awoke and found that he was not really dreaming. His body actually was crisscrossed with strong rope. His wrists and ankles were tied to the fancy, carved bedposts. And his torso was held tightly to the mattress and frame itself.

Only his head was free, and as he raised it and felt a sharp throbbing along the right temple, he saw the smiling woman at the foot of the bed.

"Hello, Raina," he said coolly. "Good to see you again."

"I am certain it is," Raina said smoothly. "Just as it was good to see me through that special mirror at the Septien Club last night."

Carter allowed himself a chuckle. "You had me all figured out, didn't you?" he said. "Except for that final bit."

Raina's smile broadened in spite of herself. "You never fail to surprise me," she said. "But no more. From now on, I take no chances. My men, the ones who tied you to this bed, are downstairs. I have only to let out a small squeal and they will come with weapons blazing." Raina kept grinning, knowing that she would triumph now.

"From when I was first broken out of prison," she said calmly in her usual soothing voice, "I have wanted to see you dead. I'd been dreaming about it for five years. I thought about it with every piece of rotten meat they served us in that hellhole. I thought of you with every bath

I never had when I was so filthy I stank like a sewer. I thought of you every time I saw a bedbug, pulled lice from my hair, watched the slightest cut become infected.

"By dawn tomorrow, Nick, Minya Stalin and General Vasco will be with me at our final destination, far beyond your sphere of influence. But of course we shall be beyond your clutches. You shall be dead."

Carter wondered what arrangement Raina had made with Giselle Mondieux. What enormous lie had Raina fed Giselle about him? Giselle had obviously called Raina to say that he was here, and then had left him to Raina and whatever plans she might have in mind. Why? It made no sense.

"Well, it's obviously your move. What are you going to do with me? Invite your cronies upstairs for some point-blank target practice?"

"I have no intention of killing you here," Raina said. "Part of my deal with Mademoiselle Mondieux was to get you out of the house so that there would be no connection between her and your untimely—or overdue, if you ask me—death."

Carter saw a ray of hope. He had been working on the ropes at his wrists since he had come awake but had made no progress. The future did not look bright. But Raina had made a promise to Giselle, and she was keeping it. In that promise lay some hope. The goons would not riddle his body with bullets while he lay trussed up in Giselle's bed. They would untie him and take him elsewhere to do the killing.

In that transition, he had to find a way to break loose. He also had to find out where Raina was going when she left Giselle's house. But first things first, and the first thing was to survive. He thanked his lucky stars that Raina would live up to her promise to Giselle. There apparently *was* honor among thieves—and killers and spies and terrorists.

"However," Raina continued, "I have had a change of heart. It will be a small inconvenience for Giselle to dispose of your body and to buy a new bed, but that's the price she must pay for befriending someone like you. I'm sorry, Nick, but I can't take the chance that you might escape while my men are taking you out to be shot elsewhere."

"Thanks," he said dryly. So much for honor. "I appreciate your apology. You've won this round, Raina. But I'm not the only one who knows what you are planning. You won't get away with your scheme. Others will stop you."

"One more word from you and I will take your own gun from the bureau over there and kill you myself. But I wish to be far from here when my men cover you with bloody little holes. Good-bye, dear Nick. You have escaped death from me four times. This time, my old friend, there is no way out for you."

Carter watched her go, knowing that she was right. The ropes on his wrists, and all across his body and on his ankles, were as tight as ever. Like Gulliver, he couldn't break the bonds that held him.

He listened as Raina, just outside the door, gave final instructions to her men.

"Wait two hours," she said. "That way, my friends and I will be on our way to the Polish lighthouse. This house must be quiet until my friends and I are on our way. And watch him closely to make certain that he doesn't get loose.''

Even as he listened to Raina walk heavily down the stairs and out of Giselle Mondieux's house, he saw seven hired thugs, each carrying a .45-caliber automatic pistol, file into the room and seat themselves in chairs around the bed. All the men had grim expressions on their faces.

As for Carter, his brain worked furiously, as did his hands and ankles.

Neither of the three areas of his body made the slightest headway on his problem.

He was, he believed, as good as dead.

SEVEN

The fire-engine-red Ferrari sped along Boulevard Ney north of the city. Giselle Mondieux, heading east away from her home in St. Cloud, was no longer crying over the loss of a man who had been special to her.

She had begun to worry.

Giselle wasn't sure whether she believed or didn't believe Carter's telling her that he worked as a bodyguard for an eccentric American billionaire. And she realized she didn't really care one way or the other. But the story told her by Raina Missou had begun to trouble her.

Nick Carter might be a charming cad or he might be the genuine article, but she found it difficult to believe that he would work for the man Raina Missou had claimed he worked for. That crazy dictator was trying to get his hands on nuclear weapons, Giselle had read in the newspapers, and he was the type who would not hesitate to use them.

Just what Nick Carter really did for a living—bodyguard or playboy—she had the feeling she'd never know. He did carry weapons, so whatever he did had to be dangerous. Could he be an agent for the U.S. or for some other government? she wondered. But she had learned enough of his idealism to know that he would not work for any man or government that did not champion the cause of the average man. She felt that Nick Carter was not the type to yearn for world domination, or to work for anyone who did.

Giselle had promised Raina Missou that she would stay away from the house all day. As she drove, she thought and worried. The more she thought, the more all the explanations given her—by both Carter and Raina—seemed farfetched.

At Avenue Jean Jaurès, Giselle left the Périphérique, the system of superhighways circling Paris, and headed back toward the city's center. At Rue La Fayette and Boulevard Haussmann, she found a public library, parked, and went inside.

She found the microfilm for a Paris daily paper for a three-month period of five years ago, when Raina Missou said that her father had been killed and that she had been wrongly imprisoned. It took five minutes to find the first article she wanted.

She read a piece that seemed more like the plot of some action/adventure thriller than events that actually happened. A group of European drug-smugglers were doing a little information-dealing as a sideline, selling state secrets from many countries to the highest bidder, usually the Soviet Union. An international team of espionage agents cornered the underworld gang on the island of Corsica in the Mediterranean, and in the bloody pursuit that followed, their leaders were killed.

Among the dead leaders was Anthony Missou, Raina's father.

Giselle continued through the microfilm, seeking additional stories. She found the one she needed in an edition a week later than the first.

Raina Missou, the story said, daughter of a deceased leader of the now disbanded underworld organization, had been turned over to Moroccan authorities by the U.S. Navy after she had boarded a U.S. aircraft carrier and had tried to kill an American diplomat. Was Nick Carter that diplomat? Giselle wondered. And was he really a diplomat, or was the U.S. Navy covering for him because he was an agent of some kind, perhaps CIA? Giselle didn't know, but she was certain now of one thing: only a part of Raina Missou's story had been true.

Nick Carter had indeed killed her father and was instrumental in having her imprisoned. But both father and daughter deserved what they had received. And Raina had used Giselle, as one wronged woman pleading to another, to get even with Nick Carter.

As she sped back toward the western edge of the city and her house near the Bois de Boulogne, she had the feeling that she would be too late. She was convinced that she would find Nick Carter dead in her bed, and it would be all her fault.

The Frenchwoman was only minutes away from being right.

Nick Carter had continued to work on his bonds, but without success. He turned his head enough to see the face of a little clock on the night table.

In just under twenty minutes, the thugs would get up from their positions around the bed, snap .45-caliber cartridges into the firing chambers of their weapons, and empty those weapons into his body.

It was almost twelve o'clock, and he suspected that Raina, Minya Stalin, and General Julio Vasco were still in Paris but would be leaving promptly at noon. They would have been on their way for at least twenty minutes by the time the bedroom in Giselle Mondieux's house would explode with the simultaneous firing of seven big automatic pistols.

And they were going, so he had overheard, to a place Raina had called "the Polish lighthouse."

For the past hour and a half, as precious time leaked away, he had pondered the mention of the lighthouse. Had Raina deliberately said it so that he would hear and go off on a wrong tack? Or if she hadn't expected him to hear and was on the level, what—and where—was the Polish lighthouse?

Was it a code name for someplace that was neither a lighthouse nor in Poland? Or should he consider the possibility that it was an actual place, a landmark, a spot in Poland? Poland's entire northern border was the Baltic Sea, and in that rocky, storm-tossed area, there were innumerable lighthouses.

Even if Raina, Stalin, and Vasco were using a remote Polish lighthouse as a central terminal for their computers, they would be unable to tap into NATO's computers

70

because NATO had safeguards against such attempts. Computer taps could be thwarted the same way that radio signals, like the Voice of America, could be jammed.

Carter still held to the idea that Minya Stalin was working without his government's sanction or knowledge. If he pulled off his plan, he'd be a Hero of the State. If he failed to pull it off, who would know?

Carter realized that all this conjecturing would get him nowhere. In just sixteen minutes, the seven goons around the bed would start the fireworks. This terrible waiting game was worse than death.

Raina Missou must have come up with one hell of a story to sway a woman of Giselle's tender temperament. Ah, it would be easy for Raina, he thought. She had probably told Giselle that her father had been murdered by Nick Carter, and that Carter had had her wrongly imprisoned. She would leave out the pertinent details and invent lots of others, and she could be one very convincing woman.

Poor, trusting, gullible Giselle. It wasn't her fault he was in this predicament. Come to think of it, he had been seeing Giselle for about five years, the same amount of time that Raina Missou had been in prison.

Raina must have known about Giselle long before Carter arrived in Paris this time. Perhaps that was one reason she lured him to Paris, knowing that if he escaped her trap, he would go to Giselle for sanctuary.

Now that it all fit together in a neat but dirty little package, what did he do with it? Carter mused. He took it to the grave with him, that's what.

In seven minutes, the firing would commence.

He quickly erased a mental image of himself being shot to death while tied to this bed in which he and Giselle had enjoyed each other's bodies so many times over the years. He thought of how it would feel when the first bullets struck. . . .

When he saw that he had only four minutes to go and that the men seated near him had looked at their watches and had stood up to mill around the room with impatience, Carter, who'd never considered himself a religious man but often thought that Someone Up There must like him considering he'd lived as long as he had and made it through some pretty hair-raising scrapes in one piece, prayed for a miracle. He figured it wouldn't hurt, and who knew . . . ?

The downstairs door opened and slammed. The seven men in the room turned as one and glared at the bedroom door that opened onto the upstairs corridor. Carter used the opportunity to glance at the clock by the bed again.

One minute until doomsday.

"Who the hell can that be?" one of the gunmen demanded of the others in English.

"Miss Missou, who else?" a second gunman responded. "Looks like she's changed her mind and didn't leave Paris like she planned."

These were the first words spoken by the gunmen, and Carter wasn't surprised by the language any more than he had been surprised by the man called Squeeze who was straight off the New York streets. Raina had somehow managed to dredge up low-level American mobsters for her dirty work.

The footfalls on the stairs were light, those of a woman.

But Carter knew it wasn't Raina. She had a different cadence. It was Giselle Mondieux. Either his prayer had been answered, or his fate had been sealed for good. He'd find out soon enough.

Giselle stormed into the room, her eyes blazing. When she saw the gunmen with their weapons drawn, and saw Nick Carter bound to the bed like a piece of furniture tied to the top of a car, she exploded in a flash of Gallic temper. It was a side of Giselle Carter had never seen. She was a woman of many surprises, he knew, but now she made him want to stand up and cheer—if only he could.

"You will not implicate me in this!" she shouted. "Mademoiselle Missou made me a promise and, by God, I expect that promise to be kept! Now, you, you and you—untie this man! I want all of you to take him out of this house immediately! Immediately, do you hear?"

The goons, accustomed to taking and following orders from anyone who sounded superior in intelligence, but remembering Raina Missou's instructions to kill Nick Carter while he was still tied to the bed, were momentarily stymied. They didn't know just what to do.

The time was down to twenty seconds.

"Don't you understand what I am saying?" Giselle screamed at the men. "I sped here in my car with the police right behind me. I eluded them a block away and parked on the street. The police are cruising the neighborhood looking for me. If you fire those big pistols, you will have them all over the house. Mademoiselle Missou promised that I would not be involved. Now, get him out of here before the police trace my license number and come here to find out who was driving that red Ferrari!"

It made sense to the criminal mind, to people who had spent a lifetime trying to elude police and collecting speeding tickets. And the goons knew that one blast from a .45 would bring police from blocks around.

The three men she had designated to do the untying were already at work. One gunman, however, still seemed dubious.

"If there're cops around," he said, "how're we gonna get this guy out of the house without them seeing? Our car is parked out on the street."

"Simple," Giselle said, more calmly now that her orders were being carried out. "One of you go down and drive the car up to the garage at the side of the house. You can take Mr. Carter out the side door and directly into the car."

"Oh, yeah. Lou, you go fetch the car. Keep an eye out for the police."

Lou nodded and went out. Carter, meanwhile, was sitting up in the bed, trying to get circulation back to various parts of his body. He watched Giselle, but she showed no interest in him. She was talking in a low voice to the gunman who'd first spoken. Suddenly she turned to the man from AXE.

"I know what you did to Raina Missou's father in Corsica, and to her in Morocco," she said to Carter, ice in her voice. "And I think I know what she tried to do to you those years ago. But none of that is my concern, and I do not want to be involved with any of this distasteful business. I merely want you out of my house. I thought you were an honorable man, Nick Carter, but I was wrong. Now I know the truth—*the whole truth*."

Carter, whose mind was reeling with plans on how to make use of this unexpected reprieve, almost missed the hidden message of Giselle's little speech. The goons missed it completely. When Carter was finally on his feet and dressed and was being marched to the doorway, Giselle reached out as though to touch his arm.

"Good-bye, Giselle," he snarled. "Thanks for nothing."

"Get this man out of my house," Giselle said to the lead gunman.

"We're doin' it, lady. Hold your horses. We're doin' it as fast as we can."

All the way down the wide staircase and out to the car Carter's mind buzzed with plans on how to break away. Nothing came to mind, and he worked on what Giselle had said upstairs.

As the car pulled away and he saw the red Ferrari parked ahead in Giselle's own garage, he knew that he was not alone, that Giselle had deliberately saved his life and planned to keep on saving it.

But what could she do? He just hoped that she had called the police before she had marched upstairs and laid down the law to Raina's bunch of imported thugs. What else was there for her to do?

Now Carter had to work out exactly what he would do.

EIGHT

Even though it was the middle of the day, the first winter storm from the North Sea had turned Paris into a city at dusk. Streetlights were on. Sleet that had changed to wet snow was sticking to the pavement and making driving slow. It was, Carter thought, a really rotten day to die.

The Killmaster was squashed between two hefty men in the rear seat of a little Renault. Two men sat in the front, and three followed in a Peugeot. Where the black Mercedes had gone with Raina Missou—and probably with her two partners in this caper—was a matter of conjecture. Carter guessed the car had gone to Orly and that the three were now aboard a plane heading to the place where the Polish lighthouse was, wherever that might be.

Carter wanted desperately to look behind them as the car made its way through the Bois de Boulogne. The park looked pretty with its light dusting of snow. Too peaceful for a killing. He hoped that behind the Peugeot would be the red Ferrari carrying Giselle Mondieux. Better yet, he hoped that Giselle had called the police and that cars with red lights on top would be following the two cars taking Nick Carter to the killing place.

The Renault neared the Hippodrome de Longchamp, the most famous racetrack in all of Europe, and Carter guessed that he would be pumped full of lead and left to spend the winter in an empty horse stall. The track had closed a month ago and would not open until April.

When the car turned off the Allée de la Reine Marguerite onto the Avenue de l'Hippodrome, he had no further doubts about his fate. A horse stall it would be for eternity, or at least until next spring. And his heart sank when the car made the turn and Carter's eyes swept to the left. He saw the Peugeot, but there was no traffic behind it, no red Ferrari and no police.

In a car with four gunmen, with another three bringing up the rear, Nick Carter felt very much alone. He was disarmed except for the little gas bomb taped high on his thigh like a third testicle. Even when he was wearing just his shorts, the men had missed Pierre. And he could think of no way to use it even if he could get to it. He wondered if this, indeed, was it.

Within seconds after the two cars carrying Carter and the seven gunmen had left, the telephone had rung in the big house of Giselle Mondieux.

"Hello, Giselle," Raina Missou had said. "I am at the airport at this moment. Our plane has been delayed because of the storm. I just called to see how things have gone with our mutual friend.''

Giselle, who now knew the truth about Raina's father and why Nick Carter had killed him and why Raina herself had been sent to prison, was in no mood for polite banter.

"You lied to me,'' she hissed into the receiver. "I know the truth."

Raina laughed. "I suppose Nick told you all sorts of stories."

"He told me nothing," Giselle spat back. "I went to the library and read all about the drugs and the spying and Corsica and your father's activities. And I know why you were sent to prison."

"I see," Raina said pensively. "Haven't you ever been told not to believe all that you read in the newspapers?"

"Do not patronize me," Giselle said. "I am going to hang up now, and I am going to call the police and let them know where you are and what your people are doing."

"And just what will you tell the police?" Raina asked, trying to sound calm but churning inside. She was so sure that meek little Giselle would follow her instructions and disappear for the afternoon. Raina never imagined that this fragile Frenchwoman might ruin everything.

"That your men are taking Nick Carter to the Hippodrome in the Bois de Boulogne to kill him," Giselle said, savoring the gasp she heard from Raina. Just before the gunmen had taken Carter down the stairs, she'd asked one of them where they'd be taking him. She was surprised that she had received an answer, but decided that these hired hands sometimes acted before they thought about the consequences; she hoped it would be one of those times. He'd told her that they were going to the Hippo-drome, which had been selected as an alternate site in case the gunmen were unable for some reason to dispose of Carter at Giselle's house. "That is your plan, isn't it? I mean, after you lied to me and planned to have Nick Carter shot here, in my own bed."

"I want to see Nick Carter dead!" Raina practically shouted. "What is he to you besides an occasional bed partner? That man took my father's life and took five years of mine!"

"But your father caused the deaths of many people in his lifetime," Giselle shot back. "I believe you tried to kill Carter and were caught in the act. Your father deserved to die and you deserved to be put in prison!"

Raina chuckled. "Your bourgeois sense of justice amuses me, Giselle. Do yourself a favor. Don't call the police. Let me explain. Part of my current plans include some extraordinarily sophisticated computers. Computers are marvelous inventions. If you know what you're doing, you can link things together more tightly and intricately than antique French lace. I didn't figure on your resource-fulness and spunk, but I didn't discount your intelligence either. Just in case you decided to return home before our need for your premises was completed, I planned a little backup precaution. I spoke of linking things? Well, should you call the police—from your house or anywhere else—I will know electronically, and your store, your home, and your body will not see this evening. Be very careful what you do in the next few minutes, Giselle. Believe me, Nick Carter isn't worth your life. *Au revoir.*"

When Giselle heard the click, indicating that Raina

Missou had hung up, the slim Frenchwoman shivered, then covered her delicate face with her hands and burst into tears.

"I will not call the police," she said to the empty room in a low, defeated voice. "I will do nothing."

The past five years, except for the brief interludes when Nick Carter had come to see her, had been bleak. And now the future looked even worse.

And there would be no Nick Carter to cheer her thoughts or to bring her occasional joy.

Carter still hadn't resigned himself to a solitary and brutal death. Had his interpretation of Giselle's words and actions been mere wishful thinking on his part that she was helping him? He hoped not. Carter let his fine mind work on the problem. As the Renault approached the Allée de Longchamp and he could see the big Hippodrome through the trees, he decided to give the gunmen something to worry about. Worry, especially the anticipation of problems in an otherwise routine—for these guys—task, could take the edge off the effectiveness of the gunmen and perhaps give that edge to Carter. It was worth a shot.

"I suppose some of your men came out earlier to pay off the men who guard the Hippodrome during the off-season," he said casually, as though resigned to the fact that the answer to his speculation had to be an unqualified "yes."

"There are no guards," the driver told him flatly. "We have been assured of that."

"Assured by Raina Missou?" Carter said, chuckling. "That's like being assured by the rattlesnake that there's no venom in those big sharp fangs. Well, it's certainly not my problem. For my part, I hope the place is crawling with armed guards waiting for us." The seeds of doubt had been planted. Now all they had to do was grow. . . .

The man in the passenger seat tapped the driver on the shoulder. "Stop on that lane to the left there," he barked. When the car was stopped and the little Peugeot behind had pulled to the side of the boulevard, near a pond, the gunman said, "Take Spencer and case the back entrance. If there are guards, give us a signal. We can either take them out or find someplace else to dump this joker."

The two men left the car, leaving tracks in the falling snow. The men in the little Peugeot got out, but the gunmen waved them back. Carter was alone in the rear seat with one gunman. In the front, with a .45 automatic aimed at Carter, was the other thug. Carter glanced out and saw that the snow was coming down more heavily now.

Carter decided that he had perhaps two minutes, no more, to make his move. And he had to do it in such a way that he didn't tip his hand to the men in the Peugeot. They had to remain ignorant of all that was happening until he was ready for them. That is, if he were ever ready for them. The wet snow had built up on the rear window of the Renault, and Carter knew it was time to move. He stuck his hands into his coat pockets.

The man in the front seat with the .45 watched Carter but figured the action was harmless. He knew that Carter had been searched for weapons, and that his Luger and stiletto were in the pockets of his comrade seated next to Carter. But he didn't know about the open seam in Carter's left pocket that let the Killmaster unfasten Pierre from its hiding place in his crotch.

Carter brought out the little egg-shaped gas bomb and held it up for the two men to see. They stared at it, disinterestedly at first and then with only slight curiosity.

"What's dat?" the gunman beside Carter asked.

"It happens to be a bomb," Carter said. He had his left thumb on the firing pin and his right hand on the window crank. He had calculated the time that he could hold his breath and the time it would take to put these men out of their misery. He knew that he couldn't hold his breath long enough, not in the closed little car, and that he couldn't set off the bomb and leap out. The men in the car behind would pick him off before he got ten feet away.

"A bomb?" the man with the .45 said. He was grinning. "You expect us to believe that?"

"Believe what you want," Carter said. He silently filled his lungs with air and turned the little bomb casually in his hand. The gunman beside him reached up to take the bomb. Carter flipped out the pin and raised the bomb to the car's ceiling.

A deadly stream of gas caught the gunman directly in the face. His hand, reaching for the bomb, halted and then dropped. Carter, still holding his breath, held the bomb out to the man in front.

And then, knowing that the detonator would blow the casing to bits and let all the compressed gas out in an instant, Carter dropped the spewing bomb on the front seat and fell to the floor in the rear. The bomb popped, and the man in front let out a yell.

Carter counted to forty and knew that he could hold his

breath no longer. The car was silent. The air in it was blue. Carter raised himself to a sitting position, saw that the two men sent to the Hippodrome to look for guards were still out of sight, and rolled down the right-side window a little. He put his lips to the crack and felt the cold Paris air. He took a gulp of clean air, then rolled up the window again.

He gave the gas another thirty seconds to make certain the two men were dead, then rolled the window all the way down. He stuck his head out and took in several lungsful of air.

The three men behind in the Peugeot had seen him stick his head out, but they had no idea of what had happened in the snow-covered Renault. Carter moved swiftly. He removed his weapons from the man who'd sat next to him. He crawled over the back of the front seat. The driver had left the engine running to keep the car warm, so there was no problem there. He took the .45 automatic from the dead gunman in the passenger seat, then heaved the man into the rear seat. He checked the outside mirror and saw that the men in the Peugeot had not made a move. Ahead, the big Hippodrome lay empty and dark in the falling snow.

Carter began to back the car up slowly, to keep the men in the Peugeot from growing suspicious. When he was within twenty feet of it, he gunned the Renault's engine and struck the Peugeot broadside. He pushed the little car over the embankment and into the shallow pond where it would take a tow truck to get it out.

And then he took off, tires spinning on snow and macadam, heading along the Allée de Longchamp toward the street that would take him to the Champs-Élysées. His final destination was the Paris office of Amalgamated Press and Wire Services. From there, he would be able to safely contact Hawk in Washington.

Carter had no intention of giving Raina Missou or her friends another crack at him now. Just how Giselle Mondieux fitted into this operation—if she did at all—he didn't know, but he knew he couldn't return to Giselle's home. Not yet, anyway.

But there were other questions that needed answering, and he hoped that Hawk would have those answers.

At the office, a pretty receptionist took him to a back room where Carter told much of what had recently happened to the agent in charge.

"You'll find two men in the backseat," Carter told the AXE agent. "They're dead—gassed. Here are the forty-fives they carried. Have someone call the gendarmes to pick up two other men at the Hippodrome, and three more stranded in a nearby pond in a Peugeot. I trust that you have replacement ammo for my Luger and a few more gas bombs for me."

"Oh, yes, indeed," the agent said. "And Hawk sent a carton of your special cigarettes. They arrived this morning."

"Thanks," Carter said. "One of those would be much appreciated. And while you're getting them, could someone get me a few sandwiches and a beer. I haven't eaten since yesterday and I'm starved."

Fifteen minutes later, Carter was attacking a ham and cheese sandwich on good crusty bread and washing it down with cold beer.

He puffed contentedly on one of his custom-blended

cigarettes with his initials embossed on the filter in gold. He had punched in his code, and people in Washington were trying to locate Hawk who was busy on another floor.

Within thirty seconds, Hawk's gruff voice was on the scrambled line. "Got anything good, N3?"

"Yes, sir, I certainly do," Carter said.

"Let's hear it."

Carter told his superior everything that had happened since Tangier.

"As for that Polish lighthouse," Hawk said when Carter had finished, "I'll have the computers do our legwork for us. We ought to come up with something useful. Are you certain the three have left Paris?"

"Yes, sir. I called Orly Airport, and three people matching their descriptions left shortly after noon on a weather-delayed flight to Stockholm. We're having a hell of a storm here, and it looks as though all the airports will soon close down."

"That doesn't leave you much time to get on their trail once we find it. Stockholm is just the first stop. I'd like to eliminate all the phony links and get to the real destination if we can."

"What have your computer checks turned up so far, sir?" Carter asked.

"About what we expected. Stalin left Russia three weeks ago and linked up with General Vasco in Tangier where they planned the prison break. Both are on leaves of absence, so we know they're not sanctioned on this trick unless that, too, is a deception. We have several addresses for them in Paris, but they're of no use to us now if they've left for Stockholm."

"Maybe not," Carter said. "While our computers in Washington are checking out a possible location for this 'Polish lighthouse,' perhaps some good old-fashioned human legwork here can turn up something. If you'll feed me those addresses, I'll check them out. You never know what you'll find that might be of value. A scrap of paper with doodling on it. Anything."

"Good thinking, N3," Hawk said between puffs on his cigar. "Call me back in two hours. And don't go off on your own before talking to me. That's an order."

"Yes, sir."

When Hawk had hung up, Carter watched the teletype deliver a lengty message in code. He deciphered the message and got the addresses he wanted. Two of them made Carter's blood chill again.

Both were on Avenue St. Cloud, and one of them was the address of Giselle Mondieux.

Carter had hoped there were extenuating circumstances that had kept Giselle from calling the police, or in helping him in another way. He had hoped against hope that she was not part of this terrible plan.

He had, he now believed, been hoping for the impossible.

NINE

A check of the Paris addresses told Nick Carter a great deal about the planning stages of the conspiracy consisting of Raina Missou, Minya Stalin, and General Julio Vasco. But it did not tell him their eventual destination.

The general from Cuba had been the first to arrive, six weeks ago, and he had lived in a small hotel on Avenue Foch, not far from the Arc de Triomphe. Within a few days of his arrival, the manager told Carter, surly-looking men who could not speak French began to show up. Carter knew that the Cuban, using ties in Miami and New York, had been the one to recruit the American thugs and gunmen.

When the group grew too large for the hotel on Avenue Foch, a house was rented on Boulevard Bineau. The landlord and the neighbors had much to say about the wild parties and the uncouthness of the group of men who lived in the house in the respectable neighborhood, but they could shed no light on where the men had gone or what their purpose in Paris might be.

Three weeks ago, the group rented a mansion on Avenue St. Cloud, three blocks from Giselle's house. At this point, Minya Stalin joined the group, and although the neighbors tried to remain aloof from the strange newcomers, they couldn't help but notice that the leader was a Spanish-speaking man with white hair and a white beard, a man who possessed great arrogance, and a man with a Russian accent whose looks were unremarkable but whose eyes "could drive a nail into an oak tree." The first, of course, was General Julio Vasco; the second had to be Minya Stalin.

The landlords of the two rented houses were cooperative, especially after Carter slipped them each a bundle of francs, but a check of the now vacated premises revealed almost nothing of value. Not even, as he had suggested to Hawk, a piece of paper with scribbling or doodling. At the house on Avenue St. Cloud, Carter found the stub of an airline ticket from Miami to Paris that had belonged to a Richard Krause. He put the stub in his pocket and continued to search the first and second floors, but he found nothing else left by its temporary occupants.

The final place to check was, of course, the home of Giselle Mondieux. Giselle couldn't know if he were alive or dead. The last she saw of him, he was being taken out to be shot elsewhere by seven thugs bearing .45-caliber pistols. She had saved him from being killed then and there, in her house, and she had seemed to offer with her eyes and her words a promise of help. When Carter had been taken from the house, he had seen Giselle's red Ferrari in the garage. The woman had lied to the gunmen, saying she had been chased by police for speeding and had parked on the street.

He wondered what had been going on in Giselle's head, and why she had done nothing after he had been led away. A brief, anonymous phone call to the gendarmes would have done it. She had only to describe the two cars bearing Carter and the seven thugs.

But she had apparently done nothing. Why?

There was no indication anywhere in his checking that tied Giselle to the assassins except the fact that three days ago, Giselle Mondieux had been visited by Raina Missou. That same day, Raina gave Giselle's address as her current residence in Paris when she cashed a traveler's check. The AXE computer network learned this interesting bit of information.

Carter figured he had only one way to find out how Giselle tied in with the conspiracy, if indeed she did. Carter headed the Renault he had rented down Avenue St. Cloud, drove past Giselle's, and saw that the red Ferrari was still in the garage. The snow, however, was falling more heavily now, and the light little Renault was having trouble turning around on the snow-clogged streets. Carter had to park a block away and walk to Giselle's house.

"Nicholas!" she gasped as she opened the front door.

"Hello, Giselle," Carter said. He looked hard at the woman. She looked as if she'd just seen a ghost.

"But you—they—I mean, how did . . ."

"It's a long story," Carter said calmly. "But to make it short, I got away and I don't think your friends are still after me. The Paris police are already rounding up the gunmen, and your three foreign pals are on the way to Stockholm.''

''What are you talking about?'' She seemed genuinely puzzled, and he noticed that her eyes were red-rimmed and swollen. He started over, explaining what had happened near the Hippodrome, and that he had learned that Raina Missou, Minya Stalin, and General Vasco had left for Stockholm in the storm.

''I almost wish their plane would go down in the storm,'' Carter muttered, moving into the den where a fire blazed merrily, ''but there are innocent people on that plane. Tell me, Giselle, why didn't they invite you along on their little junket?''

''Why would they invite me? Oh, Nicholas, do you think I am one of them?''

''Aren't you?''

''No, of course not!''

''Then why didn't you call the police after we left the house? From the way you spoke, I had the feeling you were going to try to help me.''

Giselle's eyes dropped. Carter touched her delicate chin and tilted her head up so that her large hazel eyes were looking into his.

''I asked you a question, Giselle. I want an answer.''

''Yes,'' she said, tears forming in those expressive eyes. ''I can only swear to you that I know nothing of what that woman is trying to do—other than kill you—and I am not one of her people.''

Giselle told of the visit by Raina Missou. She told Carter what Raina had told her, about how he had been ordered to kill Raina's father and had Raina imprisoned because her father had spoken out publicly against the madman for whom Carter worked.

"And because of that story," Carter said, "you betrayed me?"

"I did not know then that it was all a lie!" the woman cried. "She made me realize that I do not know very much about you. Oh, Nicholas, I am so gullible that I believe almost anything people tell me. I have always been very trusting—too trusting. When I left this house, I felt terrible. I knew something was very wrong, but I did not know what it was."

Carter listened quietly, but he didn't say anything. He just watched the pain in her face and knew that she was telling the truth.

"You must understand what was happening in my mind," Giselle pleaded through her tears. "I believed you when you told me you were a personal bodyguard to an American billionaire. How else could you explain all the weapons you carried? Mademoiselle Missou came here and told me that the bodyguard story was pure fiction, and that you were actually part of the entourage of a North African dictator who is a madman. I could see no reason not to believe her. As I said, I really don't know much about you . . ."

Carter pursed his lips and swallowed hard. He rubbed the two-day growth of stubble on his strong jaw. The woman had a good point.

"All right," he said, walking away from her and moving closer to the fire. He stared into the flickering flames for a few moments, then turned back to her. "How did you find out that Raina was lying, and why did you come roaring back here to chase the gunmen out?''

She told him of her trip to the library and of the newspaper articles she had read.

''I knew then that her father deserved to die and that she deserved to go to prison,'' Giselle said, ''but I was—and still am—puzzled about you. What are you? Those articles never mentioned your name, but I had a feeling. . . .''

''Your feelings were correct,'' Carter said gently, leveling with her for the first time and hating himself for ever having told her any untruths. His cover story, as she had said, had only made Raina's lies easier to believe. He told her what was happening. ''I can't tell you for whom I work,'' he added, ''but you can believe this: those three are hatching a plot that could cause World War Three. I have to stop them. I have some questions for you, but I'm still puzzled as to why you started out to help me and then stopped. Why didn't you call the gendarmes, Giselle? You practically signed my death warrant.''

''I know I did,'' she whispered, ''but I had no choice.''

The lovely head dropped again. Tears fell down the white cheeks, and this time Carter let her cry for a few minutes without pressing her. He lit a cigarette and stared some more at the comforting fire.

Carter finally spoke, his voice gentle. ''What happened between the time I was taken out of here and the time you decided not to do anything to help?''

''What makes you think anything happened?'' The tears were still flowing and Giselle tried to look away. She was holding something back and she couldn't look at him.

"Because of what you said and because of the way you looked at me when they were leading me out of your bedroom," Carter said. "Because of the way you reached out to touch me. I read you loud and clear, Giselle. You were telling me not to worry, that you would do something to keep me from being killed by those men. What happened to make you change your mind?"

"Miss Missou called from the airport," Giselle said, her voice cracking. "Her plane was delayed because of the storm, and she was calling to find out if you were dead. When she called, I was just reaching for the telephone to call the police. She stopped me from doing that."

"How? How did she stop you? Did she threaten you?"

Giselle dropped her eyes again, but not her head.

"Yes," she said, her voice barely above a whisper. "She told me that she had access to such a powerful computer network that she would somehow know if I called the police. She said that she would know even if I used a telephone not in this house. I do not know if such things are possible—I know about clay and glaze, not about electronics—but I was too frightened to ask just how she could learn that I was trying to help you. She threatened to blow up my store, this house, and kill me by tonight if I informed the authorities. She is a very persuasive woman." The tears were a torrent now. "I am sorry, Nicholas. I traded your life for mine."

At that moment the telephone rang. They both stared at it and then Giselle went to answer. She spoke haltingly to the party on the other end, glancing at Carter. Most of her conversation consisted of "yes" and "no." When she hung up, she said, "That was a friend who called to ask me to dinner tonight. In view of the storm and your presence, I declined.''

Carter nodded. He knew she was lying, but it didn't matter any longer. It was time to check back in with Hawk, and it was past the time when he should be actively on the trail of the three conspirators.

"I understand why you did what you did, Giselle," he said. "I understand the instinct to survive. I do not blame you for what you did; you are only human. If I survive what I must do now, I'll be back. You can count on that.''

"Must you leave now?" she asked as she followed him to the front door. "As you say, the police are taking care of the gunmen and we know that the three you seek are in Stockholm. Can't you stay with me, even for a while?"

She came into his arms, and he hesitated before embracing her. She felt like a frightened little bird, quivering against his chest. He wished that he could forget what was happening in other parts of the world and remain with this lovely woman in a corner of Paris for the night. But that was impossible.

"Stay and hold me," Giselle said. "Everything that has happened today seems like a terrible dream. I am still so frightened for you!"

"I promise you that when all this is over, I will see you again. And there will be no more stories, no more lies. You must not feel guilty about what you did. I could not have expected you to do otherwise.''

"I will wait for you," she said simply.

Carter kissed her softly on the lips, then left. The little Renault plowed through the snow to a hotel where he found a secluded telephone booth. He dialed a special number, and within seconds, Hawk was on the line.

"Having any luck, N3?" the gruff voice demanded. "What have you been doing?"

"Running down blind alleys," Carter replied. "I learned nothing here except that Giselle Mondieux isn't connected to those three. What choice tidbits have the computers come up with?"

"Some pretty good stuff," Hawk said. "Minya Stalin has another name: Andrei Stanislav. He was born in Gdynia, Poland, and was recruited by the KGB when he was a teen-ager. Gdynia is a seaport, and there are wicked rock formations offshore. There are perhaps a dozen lighthouses within twenty miles of Gdynia. The Polish lighthouse, if it's not a code name for something totally different, could be any one of them."

"And we have less than eighteen hours to find out what and where the damned place is," Carter said, glancing at his watch. "What else have you learned from the computers?"

Hawk's voice rattled on through the static caused by the storm. "There's no indication that the three have left Stockholm. The airport there closed down at one-thirty P.M., Stockholm time, but they might have arranged for a special charter service. I'm checking on that now, but it looks as though no aircraft—commercial, private, or charter—has left Stockholm since one-thirty. This storm is a major one."

Carter told his boss of his talk with Giselle Mondieux. "Just before I left Giselle a half hour ago, she got a telephone call. I know she lied about who was calling, and I have a gut feeling about that. I'll check it and call you back."

After Carter had hung up, he called the Paris offices of

Amalgamated Press and Wire Services, gave his code, and made a special request. He would have preferred to make the necessary check himself, but he doubted that the rented Renault would get him to the office in the snowstorm, and the check required the facilities available in the AXE cover office. Ten minutes later, the pay phone in the hotel rang and Carter snatched up the receiver.

"Hello."

"N3?" a voice asked.

"Yes. Proceed."

"The telephone call to the home of Giselle Mondieux was from Copenhagen, Denmark. The caller was a woman. That's all I can tell you."

"That," Carter said, fairly singing the word, "is all you need to tell me. Thanks." Carter hung up and went directly to the hotel gift shop. The shop had no maps for sale, but it did have an imitation antique wooden globe with the continents and countries etched on it. He checked the relationship between Copenhagen, Denmark, and Gdynia, Poland.

The two cities were seacoast ports in the southern part of the Baltic Sea. They were approximately 250 miles apart. With airports closed throughout Europe now, the only way the three conspirators could get to the Polish coastline, if indeed that was their destination, was by boat. Carter felt surer by the minute that the "Polish lighthouse" was exactly that. And the Baltic had to be a raging beast by now.

As for Carter, he was hampered by the same storm.

He sat in the warm hotel lobby and pondered the problem. He knew that there was only one option, and that it was a dangerous one. The biggest problem would be in convincing the proper authorities of the necessity of his plan, and then implementing it in the teeth of the worst November storm in Europe's history.

Raina Missou came into the cozy hotel bar and spotted the Cuban general and the Russian KGB man sitting at a table near the roaring fireplace. She shook snow from her fur coat and strode past diners to the table by the fire.

"Well, gentlemen," she snapped as she gazed at their dry clothes and warm faces, "while you've been sitting here drinking wine and soaking up heat, I've accomplished what you both said was impossible."

"You've found a boat?" General Vasco asked. The fingers of his right hand played with his beard, occasionally touching the scar on his neck. It was a nervous habit that irritated Raina.

"And a captain crazy or stupid enough to take it out?" Minya Stalin added.

"I have," Raina said as she shook more melting snowflakes from her luxurious fur and draped the coat over the back of a chair. "The captain may be crazy, but he is far from stupid. He has a specially designed fishing boat that can make it through seas that are very rough. He has sailed in storms twice as bad as this one and—"

"And he tells tall tales like every other sailor in the world," Minya Stalin interjected. "From what we have heard from others in the bar here, there has not been a storm as bad as this one in recent memory, and no captain who knows the seas would venture out in it. Face it, Raina, our plans must be delayed a day or two."

"There can be no delay," Raina said. "That stupid woman in Paris interfered at the last moment. Carter is alive. I know he was with her when I called. I made her too frightened to lie. He's probably had the call traced already and knows where we are. We must leave as soon as possible. The boat will be ready to take us within six hours. And, ah, here is our captain now."

A tall blond man with blue eyes walked unsteadily through the restaurant and came up to the table where the two men and the woman sat. Raina noticed for the first time that the whites of the captain's eyes were laced with red veins. *Christ,* she thought, *the man is drunk. No wonder he agreed to take us out in this storm.*

"Gentlemen," Raina said, keeping her voice even, "this is Captain Lars Norrstrom, owner and captain of the *Little Mermaid*. Captain Norrstrom, meet my associates. This is Señor Santiago from Peru, and Herr Stanislav, formerly of East Germany. He is the one who wishes to return to his home island of Rügen, off the East German coast."

"I see," the captain said thickly as he yanked out a chair and folded his lanky form into it. He took off his wool cap and revealed a great shock of yellow hair that was streaked with white. The man was easily sixty, the three guessed, but he had the bearing and appearance of strength of a much younger man. "Well, for the right price, I don't care where he wants to go. The *Little Mermaid* is capable of getting him there, even in this weather, if he so desires. But for now, we wait. The storm will let up in one hour. I know."

"And how do you know this?" Minya Stalin demanded.

THE ASSASSIN CONVENTION

"Experience," Captain Norrstrom said. He motioned for the waiter. "Trust me. I know this sea the way a husband knows the hairs of—ah, here is the waiter. Glög for me. I cannot speak for the others."

An hour later, after the Danish captain had swallowed a half gallon of the hot, spiced wine and was still bragging about how well he knew the sea and how incredible his boat, the *Little Mermaid,* was, the storm raging down across the Baltic had increased in intensity.

From the front window of the hotel, only a few yards from the harbor, Raina Missou could not even see the boats at the docks because of the falling snow. There was no visibility. It was as if white shutters had been closed before the windows.

"One more hour," Captain Norrstrom said with that dead certainty of the drunk. "In one more hour the storm will cease altogether, and we shall set sail, or engine, if you prefer, for the sunny shores of Rügen." He toasted the falling snow with still another glass of hot wine.

"Oh, shut up," Minya Stalin snarled.

Stalin was particularly angry because he carried with him the necessary digits of the code, digits that would counteract NATO's thwarting or jamming of computer orders from Iron Curtain countries.

Without Stalin's critical input, the cruise missile could not be fired.

TEN

Before Carter checked back in with Hawk, he studied the airline stub he had found at the mansion on Avenue St. Cloud. He was sitting in the phone booth of the hotel lobby. Outside, the storm had grown worse, and he knew that the Renault was useless for the duration. It was probably buried by now.

On a hunch, he called a police inspector he knew on the Paris force. Some years ago, a Soviet spy had penetrated the French *Sûreté* and was feeding valuable data back to Moscow. Inspector Claude Chardeau was one of only a few French authorities who knew of Carter's role in identifying the mole, and was indebted to him.

"Inspector Chardeau," the crisp voice of his old friend rattled through the phone line.

"Hello, Claude. Nick Carter here. Are you in the mood to do an old buddy a favor?"

"Anything that won't take me out into this storm," Chardeau said amiably. "What is it you wish, *mon ami*?"

"I think your people have an American prisoner by the name of Richard Krause. He was arrested this afternoon in the Bois de Boulogne. He flew here under that name, but it's most likely an alias. He's probably staying with Krause and has papers to prove it."

"Let me check," Chardeau said. There was a rustle of papers, then the distant voice of Chardeau talking on another telephone. He was quickly back with Carter. "He's here," the inspector said. "Central Prison, Cell Block J. Do you want to visit him?"

"Not in this storm," Carter said. "First, tell me what he's charged with."

"Possession of firearm, resisting arrest, entering the country with a false passport—plus a few other small things that will keep him here for a time. He is under a million-franc bail."

"Has anyone come to bail him out?"

"Not a soul."

"Okay. Is it possible to have him brought to your office so that I can talk to him on the phone?"

Inspector Chardeau sighed and groaned. "When you ask a favor, my friend, you really ask a favor. It is possible, but the paperwork is a pain in the derrière."

"I know it is," Carter said apologetically. "But this really is important, Claude, and I don't have proper transportation to get to Central Prison. Will you have him brought up and call me at this number?"

"*Oui, mon ami*. For you, I will do it."

Carter gave the inspector the number of the pay telephone, lit up one of his special cigarettes, and gazed through the lobby window at the snow. Cars were stuck in every conceivable position on the boulevard outside. People walked as though going uphill, their coat collars turned up against the wind. Their hats were covered with snow, and even those who were bundled up looked cold and miserable. Every so often the snow would come horizontally, directly into pedestrians' faces.

The storm, he knew, had caused the Missou-Stalin-Vasco trio to alter their plans. He guessed that they were in Copenhagen right now trying to find a boat to take them to Gdynia. And he guessed that their chances of accomplishing this were at present quite impossible. Then again, his chances of reaching Copenhagen were equally dismal.

Unless, of course, he could get help from AXE. His plan to reach Copenhagen depended a great deal on land transportation, if only for a relatively short distance. He snatched up the telephone and called the nearest car rental agency to ask for a four-wheel-drive vehicle. The agency had two left, but they would be rented on a first-come, first-served basis. Carter fished one of many credit cards from a folder in his breast pocket, read off the number, and rented a Land-Rover. He would have to walk ten blocks through the storm to pick it up, but he was glad a car was available.

As soon as he hung up from renting the Land-Rover, the phone rang. He grabbed the receiver.

"Nick? This is Claude. I have your man here. He claims his real name is Anthony Caruso, but it doesn't matter."

Carter talked to the gunman for several minutes, determining that he was one of the three men in the Peugeot that Carter had shoved into the shallow pond near the Hippodrome de Longchamp. At first, the vague answers to Carter's questions netted nothing of interest, but then it dawned on the prisoner that the American he was talking to must have incredible influence with the Paris police, and he began to volunteer information.

"All I know for sure," he said, "is that nobody can stop those three. They got a hotshot computer expert who used to work for NATO, name of Steiner. I talked with the guy once when they had the experts hangin' out at the hotel on Avenue Foch. He said he'd been to the lighthouse off Gdynia and didn't want to go there no more. Said it was on the east side of the breakwater that runs out from the harbor, and that the winds and waves were worse there than anywhere else. Say, buddy, considerin' I'm talkin' and all, helpin' the law, d'you think you could put in a good word for me with the Paris fuzz?"

"I could," Carter said, "but I'd only have to keep looking over my shoulder for you and that big forty-five."

"Hey, listen, pal, I was just doin' a job for a whole lot of dough. I ain't got no loyalties to nobody, and the deal's off now that the broad who hired me has skipped off to Stockholm, or maybe she's on that island off East Germany by now."

"What island?" Carter asked, his interest picking up.

"Called Rügen or something like that," the man replied. "They were gonna fly there from Copenhagen and get picked up by a Polish warship for the final leg. At least, that's what this guy Steiner told me. Steiner didn't seem too hot on the idea, so I figure they got something on him to keep him in line."

When Inspector Claude Chardeau was back on the phone, Carter said, "If you can, Claude, let the guy go. Without a weapon, and with the streets jammed with snow and stalled cars, he's no threat to me. He just might make it back to the States and you'll never hear of him again. Otherwise, the French government will be feeding the bastard for years."

"I'll see what I can do," Chardeau replied. "Did his information prove of some help?"

"Some," Carter said noncommittally. "Thank you, Claude. Someday I'll explain what all this is about. Now I owe you a favor. Call on me anytime."

The inspector sighed and groaned again. "Easier said than done," he said. "Calling on you is like calling on the stars. Even if you know where they are, you just can't seem to reach them. Take care, Nick."

"I will. As for Caruso, or whatever his name is, keep him at least three more hours. When it comes to trouble, I don't trust anyone."

"Right. *Au revoir, mon ami.*"

"Good-bye, Claude."

Carter dialed the special number in Washington, D.C., and soon had David Hawk on the line. He quickly related what had happened since their last conversation. He told him that he'd learned that Raina Missou had telephoned Giselle from Copenhagen, not Stockholm, and that he now believed more than ever that the phrase "Polish lighthouse" meant just that. He described his talk with the hired American hoodlum held by the Paris police. But Carter knew that his mention of Rügen, the island off the East German coast, was what really worried Hawk.

"If they get to Rügen," Hawk said, "we're in big

trouble. If that Polish warship picks them up, things are going to get very sticky. You've got to stop them in Copenhagen, N3, and stop them for good.''

Carter told him of his plan to get to Copenhagen. It involved using a military jet assigned to NATO. "I'll have no more than the usual trouble getting to the base from here,'' Carter assured his boss. "I've managed to rent a Land-Rover, and I'm praying that the major roads are being kept more-or-less passable.''

"And just how is that blizzard?'' Hawk demanded. "You know, N3, all flights—commercial, private, and charter—are canceled throughout most of Europe east of the Pyrenees.''

"True. But military and spy planes are slicing through this mess. You know as well as I do that Allied security measures go on regardless of the weather. Neither snow nor sleet nor rain, etc., will keep NATO espionage flights from their appointed rounds and all that.''

Hawk chuckled. "Point well made and taken, Nick. I'll see what I can do about getting you a plane.''

"All you have to do is ask, sir,'' Carter said. Flattery never hurt, he mused.

"I hope it'll be that easy,'' Hawk said, then hung up.

Carter hung up slowly and contemplated the hours ahead while he waited for Hawk to get back to him about his using a military jet to reach Copenhagen.

All in all, this was not turning out to be one of his favorite trips to Paris.

The man called Squeeze had been watching the man on the telephone for quite some time now. He was in a far corner of the hotel lobby, behind a column, and he was pretending to sleep with a newspaper over his face. He had torn a slit in the newspaper so that he could see what went on around him, and he felt a crazy sense of justice when Carter entered.

Squeeze had decided that Carter meant what he said the previous evening, and decided to make himself scarce after Carter let him run from the alley. Carter's walking into the hotel at which he'd registered was one of those bizarre coincidences that Squeeze prayed for. And cabin fever had gotten him down from his small room into the lobby. He'd chosen to leave Carter alone, and Carter came to him. It made one almost Believe.

The little gangster held no hatred for the man who had questioned him in that dark street after they'd walked from the George V. He had fully expected the man to kill him and leave him there. It surprised him that not every man used Squeeze's more brutal methods of interrogation.

But Carter hadn't killed the wiry little man from Brooklyn, and the little man hadn't earned his nickname idly. He was called Squeeze because of his cunning ability to squeeze in and out of tight scrapes. He had lived forty-six years by his wits and accumulated street smarts. He looked forward to at least as many years.

And now, with the man he had been paid to watch coming into the very hotel in which he had sought refuge, his luck had turned full circle. He had some information to sell this man whose death he'd almost caused. He would gladly give the information for free, since Carter could easily have killed him but hadn't, but he needed cash. Raina Missou had defaulted on her final payment to him and had even threatened his life if he caused any trouble about it. All he wanted was money to get home. He had it with everyone connected to this job and the rotten weather was the capper.

For now, Squeeze needed Carter, and whether he knew it or not, Carter needed Squeeze.

The ferretlike little man put down his paper, ran a finger through his dirty salt-and-pepper hair, and walked boldly across the lobby and stopped near the man who seemed to be waiting for another phone call.

"How's it goin', Mr. Carter?" Squeeze said jovially, by way of greeting. "Bet you're surprised to see me again, aren't you?"

Carter spun around, recognizing the voice. He smiled when he saw the little man called Squeeze. "Surprised isn't the right word," Carter said lightly. He trusted his gut reaction that the man was no threat to him now.

"I hope the word is 'glad,' " Squeeze replied, " 'cause I got some dope you ought to have."

Carter decided that Squeeze, a hood from the old school, meant information rather than narcotics.

"Okay. Spill it."

"Hey, it ain't that easy, man," Squeeze said, holding his hands out in a placating gesture. "You know, I got left here high and dry. Like broke. That lady with the black hair who wanted you dead paid me half my freight, and I spent it on booze and dames. This is some town. Anyway, she skipped out on the second half, and I ain't got the price of cab fare to the airport, much less the bread to get me a ticket back to the Big Apple. You think you can spare a few hundred bucks to see me through to home? I guarantee the dope I got'll be worth every penny to you."

"I don't carry that much cash," Carter replied. "But what I can do is call a friend, an American newspaperman working in Paris. He owes me a bundle. I can give you a note and tell him to give you plane fare, plus a few bucks for general expenses. That make it with you?"

"In spades," Squeeze said, grinning from ear to big ear. "You call the guy and write the note, then I'll give you the dope."

"Just reverse the procedure and we have a deal," Carter said.

"Compromise," Squeeze said, still grinning. "Call the guy but don't write the note until I give and you buy. Okay?"

"Just start talking. When this telephone rings the next time, your information might not be worth a plugged nickel to me."

Squeeze figured he had nothing to lose. He gazed around the lobby to make certain they weren't being observed. "You ever hear of a computer expert name of Neil Steiner, works for NATO and is based in Brussels?"

"I've heard of Steiner," Carter admitted. "What about him?"

"Well, he's got his nuts in the ringer, kind of, and is doing a job for the lady and her buddies to save his family's life."

"What does Steiner's family have to do with this?" Carter asked.

"Missou had Steiner's family brought down from Brussels to Paris a week ago, when Steiner told her he didn't want to go through with the plan. They put the

111

family—wife and three kids—in a subbasement of the house on Avenue St. Cloud. Far as I know, they're still there. The deal is, if Steiner cooperates, his family will be freed. If he doesn't, they'll be wiped out. Oldest schtick in the books.''

Dammit, Car thought. He was in that house and was sure it was empty. He'd automatically checked the basement, too, even though every indication was that the group staying there had spent all their time on the upper floors. He hadn't suspected that a private residence would have something as unusual as a subbasement.

"Let me ask you something," Carter said. "Is the family under guard?"

"I don't know. They were supposed to be, but it looks like all the brass and the goons have either flown the coop or been picked up by the Paris cops. If there are guards, they'll blow you to hell when you show up. If there ain't no guards, I wouldn't bet that Steiner's wife and three kids are still alive."

"They would have killed them before they left?" Carter asked, his voice grim.

"Hell, no," Squeeze said. "They'd leave 'em to starve. That woman and her pals were hard as nails."

Carter made his call to the Amalgamated Press Offices, then wrote a note authorizing his "friend" to pay Squeeze a thousand dollars in francs. He gave the little man the note and told him not to spend an extra minute in Paris, but to hotfoot it to the airport and get in line for the next flight out.

As Carter was trying to decide whether to pick up the Land-Rover he had rented and check the abandoned mansion on Avenue St. Cloud, the telephone rang. It was, of course, Hawk.

"The jet will be ready as soon as you arrive," the AXE chief advised. "I had to pull some very big strings on this deal, so don't blow it, N3. Be there."

"Anything new on the location of the Polish lighthouse?" Carter asked.

"A little. ComSat satellites have observed a Polish destroyer coming and going to and from one at Point Lochsa, twenty miles northeast of Gdynia. I'd say it's our target. And you can thank your friend Caruso for tipping us that the lighthouse was on the east side of the harbor. I hope you did the boy a favor."

"I did," Carter said. "He's getting his wings in three hours, after I'm long gone from Paris."

"You'd better be out of there faster than that," Hawk said. "The jet's waiting for you."

Carter told his boss of a slight detour he had to make to the house on Avenue St. Cloud. "I have to do this myself. I could send the police, but I have to know before I leave here that the Steiner family is all right. Besides, I have an ulterior motive."

"What's that, Nick?"

"I may have a chance to get to Steiner before the others do, at the lighthouse. Can you have an American ship pick me up in Copenhagen?"

There was a good deal of muttering and puffing on a cigar on the line from Washington, then Carter continued.

"If I can get to him first, I'd like to have in my possession a note from Mrs. Steiner saying that she and the children are safe. I've already decided on a place to stash them. With the note and the good news, maybe I can swing Steiner around and get his cooperation."

"It might be worth a try, but having an American ship so close to the Polish border while there's a Polish warship in the same neighborhood could push us very close to the edge."

"Yes, sir, I realize all that. I also realize that the firing of a cruise missile at a Russian target will take us over the edge."

"That's true, but can anyone guarantee that getting to Steiner will cancel this operation? He's probably only one link in a long chain. He couldn't stop this firing even if he wanted to."

"Granted, but he could change the target."

"That's a possibility. Good thinking, Nick."

"Steiner could secretly program the cruise missile to head for the Atlantic Ocean," Carter said, grinning into the receiver. "Now, who behind the Iron Curtain could possibly object if a cruise missile is fired at an empty spot in the Atlantic Ocean? Especially if we have proof that computers located on Polish soil did the firing?"

There was a pause. "Get going," Hawk finally said. "But make it snappy. Tomorrow morning is coming up fast, storm or no storm. I'll start arranging for a U.S. ship to take you aboard in Copenhagen."

"Thanks, sir. I'll do my best."

"I know, Nick. That's all I ever hope for."

ELEVEN

It was a long, cold ten blocks.

The storm had been worsening by the hour, and the wind from the northeast cut through Carter's coat and seemed to go right into his bones. Snow accumulated on his dark eyebrows and on the stubble that covered much of his face. His hair was white.

He caught a glimpse of himself in a shop window and realized he looked like Frosty the Snowman in a trench coat.

But he made it to the car rental agency with some feeling still left in his fingers and toes, and completed the paperwork for renting the Land-Rover.

Ten minutes after he left the office, he was plowing through the snow-filled Paris streets. The vehicle was running smoothly and it was warm inside. Carter had no trouble maneuvering the Jeep-like car through the snow; it was the stalled conventional vehicles that made the going slow. And the police, wanting to keep certain streets cleared for emergency vehicles, kept stopping him and trying to turn him back. He assured them that the Land-Rover would not get stuck and clog the street ahead.

He passed Giselle Mondieux's house on his way up Avenue St. Cloud, but he could not see the garage or the red Ferrari through the tumbling snow. Snow had covered all the windows, and the windshield wipers battled valiantly against the swirling ice and snow. Carter had to stop a number of times to break the ice off the wipers with his bare hands.

He cursed the storm, recalling the pleasant weather in Tangier. Was that only a few days ago? he thought; the past forty-eight hours had been a blur. He even wished for the sleet and rain that had greeted him on his arrival in Paris. By comparison it had been wonderful.

The huge house that had been rented and occupied by Raina Missou and her cronies stood stark and empty against a dark afternoon sky that was filled with storm clouds and curtains of falling snow. Carter nudged the Land-Rover into the drifts at the driveway entrance, backed up, revved the engine, and plowed his way to the carport at the side of the house. Piles of heavy wet snow had already filled the carport and half buried the three steps to the side door.

He got out and was met by a gust of icy wind that slammed his heavy frame back against the side of the vehicle. He cursed aloud, but the howling wind swept away his words.

Carter climbed the steps and tried the door off the

carport. It was locked, so he snapped Hugo into his hand and went to work on the lock. The longer it took, the colder he got, and the colder he got, the longer it took. Finally the door was open, and Carter stepped inside the first-floor hallway, his Luger going first in his outstretched hand.

The bone-chilling coldness of the house convinced him that no one was in the upper floors. The mansion was like a meat locker. When he'd been there earlier he remembered that the furnace was on in the basement, and it was reasonably warm down there. He figured that the heat was off in the main part of the house, but the furnace had been kept on so the water pipes wouldn't freeze. Then again, maybe it was on so any men guarding the Steiners wouldn't freeze.

Yet Carter had seen and heard no one on his previous visit. Had any guards there figured that Madame Steiner and her brood were securely locked up and it was safe to duck out somewhere for a bite to eat?

Carter found the door to the basement and opened it slowly. This time he knew that he was not alone. He heard heavy footsteps and, when he listened carefully, the muted sound of children crying. Had the frightened family been asleep when he'd checked the basement earlier that day? He didn't dare go down the stairs to the basement and quietly closed the door. He backtracked to the door opening onto the carport and went back into the storm. He circled the big house, searching for a window that looked into the basement.

He located a small window that had been covered by a snowdrift. He figured the guard or guards would not be watching that window, but would be concentrating on windows that gave an unobstructed view out of the basement. Carter slowly cleared away the snow, and gritting his chattering teeth, he took off his trench coat and used it to cover the window, blocking out any light.

Working slowly and patiently, despite the bitter cold, Nick Carter used the diamond-hard tip of his stiletto to etch a square in the window glass. Over and over he worked the tip in the outline. Then, when he felt that the glass had been weakened sufficiently, he covered the stiletto handle with his folded handkerchief and tapped lightly. The small square gave way, but the frozen fingers of his left hand managed to catch it before it could hit the floor inside. Turning the cut-out piece at an angle, he slipped it out through the small opening, then reached in and unlatched the window. He opened the window under the cover of his coat, slipped inside as silently as a cat, and leaving the coat outside to keep the window dark, closed the window just as quietly. He thanked his lucky stars for the noise of the wind.

Carter moved through the dimly lit basement, Hugo and Wilhelmina at the ready. He found the first guard squatting behind the furnace. The man had an AK-47 rifle pointed at the staircase and was staring almost hypnotically in that direction. Carter moved like a shadow and passed Hugo's blade across the man's throat. There was a soft gurgle as the man died. Carter dragged the body to a corner so that his blood wouldn't leak out past the furnace.

A second guard was beneath the stairs. Carter made him by taking the first guard's place and waiting. After ten minutes, the guard beneath the stairs poked out his head and looked toward the furnace.

"Mike, you still there?" the man asked, fear in his voice.

"Yeah," Carter replied, coughing as he said it to disguise his voice.

"I know there was somebody up there. I heard footsteps and heard the goddamned door open and close. Now I don't hear nothin'. Do you, Mike? Where the hell did he go?" A child let out a small cry just then, saving Carter having to answer.

"Jesus, them's the cryingest kids I ever heard," the man under the steps complained. "The lady, too. They just sit around alla time in the fruit cellar cryin' and cryin'. It's drivin' me nuts! Well, it won't be long now before the two of us can get out of here, eh, Mike? Miss Missou said dawn tomorrow and we could do what we want with 'em. What should we do with 'em, d'ya think? Hey, Mike, say somethin'."

"Mike" had heard enough. The Killmaster stepped from behind the furnace with his Luger aimed at the man beneath the stairs.

He squeezed the trigger and watched grim-faced as the man screamed, clutched his chest, and collapsed beneath the basement stairway, a look of great surprise on his ugly face. Then Carter ran toward the sound of children crying, toward a small door near the base of the stairs. The door was not locked, and he opened it and called down in his calmest voice.

"Madame Steiner, it's all right. My name is Carter and I'm a policeman"—he thought that sounded reassuring under the circumstances—"and I've come to get you out of here. The guards are dead. Get your children and come up the stairs. I'll come down and help you."

He began to walk down into the dark subbasement and was met halfway down by a woman in her mid-thirties, followed by two boys and a little girl. Beneath the terror in her eyes and the dirt on her face and arms, Carter could see that she was very beautiful, with blond hair and huge blue eyes. The children also had the startlingly blue eyes and yellow hair of their mother. They looked thin and tired, their faces hollow, their eyes red and puffy. They had no coats, and their skin was covered with goose bumps. The little girl, who looked to Carter to be about five, clung to her mother. But the older boy approached Carter with his right hand out.

"Thank you, sir, for rescuing us. I am Peter Steiner and this is my brother Jan." Jan, about eleven, came forward shyly and looked up at Carter as if he couldn't believe he was out of that freezing, stinking fruit cellar. Carter realized what a nightmare it must have been for the little family. "That's Lisette," Peter added, pointing to the small girl.

"And I'm Helen Steiner," the woman said in a low, melodious voice. "Will you please tell us who did this to us and why? These are children, for heaven's sake! They hardly fed us, there was no heat, there was no toilet, they didn't give us as much as a blanket—" She stopped, biting her lip to keep from crying, from screaming her anger. Now that the danger was past, she was letting her rage spill forth. "What is going on, Monsieur Carter? Is Neil all right? First my husband disappears, and then this . . . Oh, my God . . ."

Now Peter and Jan put their arms around their mother, and Carter let them all cry together in relief. He went to retrieve his coat from the window, hoping they wouldn't see the bodies of the guards.

"Come, Madame Steiner, you and your family need warmth and food and hot baths. Then we'll work on answers to your questions."

Helen Steiner seemed to accept this, and herded her children up the stairs and out to the carport, where they climbed into the Land-Rover. Soon the heater was sending out warm air, and the children looked better already. The snow was still coming down, but soon they were slowly traveling the short distance to Giselle Mondieux's house.

"Where are we going?" Helen Steiner asked Carter after a few blocks.

"To the home of a friend where you'll be safe," Carter replied. "If you think the children need medical attention, there is a hospital nearby . . ."

"Oh, no, Monsieur Carter. Some warmth, food, and sleep, and we'll all be fine. The children will probably want to go and play in the snow tomorrow." She paused, running her fingers through Lisette's hair. The little girl was sitting on her lap, her nose pressed to the window. "Who are you, *monsieur?* Why are we going to someone's house and not to police headquarters? We were kidnapped, after all."

Carter realized that her ordeal had made her suspicious, and he could easily understand her reaction. He had to calm her before she panicked.

"I'm not a regular Paris policeman, Madame Steiner. Let's just say that I work for an international law enforcement agency, and I want you and your children to be safe.

Please understand that that's all I can tell you right now. It's a long story, and I hope the final chapter will be over very soon." He turned and looked at his passenger. She nodded and gazed out the window.

Carter stopped the car in front of an elegant town house. "We're here, everybody. A very lovely lady lives here, and she'll see that you are comfortable. Her name is Giselle Mondieux."

At the mention of the name, Helen Steiner gasped and clutched Lisette to her tightly.

"Oh, no! She is one of them! I heard them speak of her! You must be one of them, too! This is a trick—" She seemed ready to bolt from the car into the storm.

Carter grabbed her arm. "She is not one of them. They used her for their own purposes, then threatened to kill her if she called the authorities. Believe me, she has nothing to do with these people and what they are up to. I am telling you the truth. Come, let's go meet her."

Giselle Mondieux was sitting in front of a roaring fire drinking a cup of coffee when she heard the car stop outside. She got up and looked out the front window. In front of the house was a red Land-Rover, and she watched, puzzled, as two blond boys tumbled from the back seat and ran up the stairs to her front door. From the front passenger seat came a tall, thin, exhausted-looking woman carrying a little girl. But her puzzlement turned to astonishment when she saw who stepped from the driver's side. Nick Carter.

She ran to the door and opened it, ushering her half-frozen guests inside. She was so surprised she was speechless.

"Giselle Mondieux," Carter said formally when they were all in the warm foyer, "this is Helen Steiner and her children Peter, Jan, and Lisette. They have been prisoners of Raina Missou and her friends. They are hungry and cold and tired, and I couldn't think of a better place to bring them."

Giselle immediately aimed them toward the den and sat the children in front of the fireplace. Ignoring Giselle's protests that she'd do it herself, Helen Steiner helped her put together a tray of food from the refrigerator.

When the two women returned from the kitchen with the food and cups of steaming coffee, and hot chocolate for the children, they found Carter in an armchair before the fire sipping a cognac. Peter, Jan, and Lisette were sound asleep on the carpet at his feet.

After a few minutes, Carter looked directly at Helen Steiner. "I can't stay much longer, so I'll get right to the point. Why is your husband working for Raina Missou?"

Helen Steiner shook her head sadly. "I don't know much about it," she said, and Carter believed her. "Neil told me several months ago that he had an opportunity to make a great deal of money. We had debts, Monsieur Carter, but that is not important. Later, Neil seemed afraid, but he said it was too late to turn back. And then he went away, and some terrible people came to our house in Brussels and brought us to Paris and placed us in that horrible cellar. Can you tell me what Neil is doing?"

Carter glanced down at his drink, then looked up at the two women.

"Madame Steiner, your husband has gotten himself involved with some international terrorists who, if they aren't stopped, could—at the very least—destroy the Free

World, and at worst could start a nuclear holocaust that would doom the entire world. They are using your husband's expertise with computers to accomplish their ends. And I must be on my way to try and stop them. Giselle will tell you as much as I know about their plans. I'm sorry I can't explain it myself, but I have a jet waiting for me. I'm going to try and find your husband and stop this madness caused by three insane people.'' He paused. ''Before I go, Madame Steiner, I'd like you to give me a note saying that you and the children are free and well. Perhaps if I reach him in time, it may help convince him not to do what he has been ordered to.''

A few minutes later, Giselle walked him to the front door. She'd found a muffler, some wool gloves, and a wool ski hat for Carter, and the drink and the fire had thawed him out.

''Thank you, Giselle,'' he said, drawing her into his arms, ''for everything. Take care of them, and of yourself. My promise still holds. I'll be back as soon as I can.'' He noticed that she was crying. ''Don't be scared. It'll all be over very soon.'' He kissed her wet cheeks and then her lips. She clung to him and shuddered.

''*Au revoir, mon cher*. Good luck.''

Carter waved as he walked down the stairs and into the snow toward the car.

He'd need it.

''One more hour,'' Captain Lars Norrstrom said thickly as he raised another glass of wine to his lips. ''Believe me, good people, the storm will cease in one more hour.''

Around the table by the fireplace in the little hotel bar at the wharf in Copenhagen, Raina Missou, Minya Stalin, and General Julio Vasco watched and listened to the drunken captain who had been promising a break in the weather "in one hour" for the past three hours, and all the while getting more and more drunk.

"This is ridiculous," Stalin finally said. "The ship that I have arranged to pick us up at Rügen will be there at nine o'clock. It will wait for three hours only and then will depart with or without us. If we do not arrive in time, the captain of the Polish destroyer will proceed to duties elsewhere in the Baltic Sea, and our chance of reaching the lighthouse will be lost."

"I know," Raina agreed. "But what can we do?" She knew that the captain of the Polish ship was taking a big chance by going to Rügen to pick up the conspirators and taking them to the lighthouse near Gdynia. The captain was a childhood friend of Minya Stalin, and he'd decided that a few hours' detour would not make his superiors too suspicious. And now the terrible weather and rough seas provided a good excuse for any delay; he wouldn't get in trouble.

"For one thing," Stalin said, "we can sober up your prize find here." He looked at the Danish captain with disgust. "If this storm ever does let up, at least we'll have a man capable of getting us to Rügen in time."

"I'll order coffee," Raina suggested.

"No good," General Vasco interjected. "I have learned from experience that coffee does not sober up a man. It merely produces a very alert and very wide-awake drunk."

"Then, what do you suggest?" Stalin demanded impatiently. He was clearly angry.

"We start with a cold shower, then we use some of those marvelous drugs you carry around in your attaché case," the general said. "Come, help me with this big oaf."

Stalin and Vasco got up from the table and flanked Norrstrom's chair, then each man grabbed the big sea captain by his upper arms.

"What, what?" Captain Lars Norrstrom protested when the two men hoisted him from his chair by his armpits. "What are you doing?" His voice, thick with wine and indignation, was loud and his words were slurred, but the three who had been seated with him did not care if they caused a scene. Despite the captain's protests, Stalin and General Vasco half dragged, half carried him up the stairs of the inn to one of the two rooms they had taken just in case the storm kept them there all night.

Somehwere along the way, the big captain passed out and became over two hundred pounds of dead weight. It took all three of them, plus all their energy, to haul him into a bathroom. They stripped down to his shorts, then pulled him into the bathtub. Norrstrom was still out cold. Raina pulled the torn plastic shower curtain closed, then turned on the faucet.

The shower of cold water brought a whoop and a shout and a stream of curses from the drunken captain, then the man settled beneath the cascade like a corpse, no longer feeling anything. Minya Stalin gave the Dane a shot of vitamins, followed by a dose of amphetamines. Within a short time, the big captain was dancing around the room. He was, as General Vasco had predicted, a very alert and very wide-awake drunk.

"Let us go! Let us sail!" Captain Norrstrom shouted as he stomped around the room and peered out the window at the blizzard. "The storm is no threat to us now. I can sail through this in a canoe, my friends. Believe me, I can! But first, let us have some more wine."

"No more wine," Minya Stalin said firmly, aiming Norrstrom toward the bathroom. "You need another cold shower. When the storm does let up, we leave this place. Time is running out."

Time was also running out for Nick Carter. He had to drive to a NATO base near the Belgian border to get the plane that Hawk had arranged to take him to Copenhagen. The highway was clogged with snow and disabled automobiles. He felt fortunate when he was able to nudge the Land-Rover up to twenty miles an hour.

What would ordinarily have been a two-hour drive once out of Paris was turning into an afternoon of horror. The only vehicles that moved faster than the Land-Rover were occasional snowmobiles that ripped along the shoulder of the road or through the snow-covered fields, their tiny headlights illuminating the thickly falling snow.

Suddenly, Carter's eyes were caught by a slight movement from the dashboard. The gas gauge needle had moved just enough for Carter's peripheral vision to pick it up.

It was near the empty mark.

Between running around Paris rescuing the Steiner family and the slow going on the highway, he'd gone through a tank of gas. And he hadn't noticed an open gas station for the last hour.

He moved onward, his nervous eyes watching the gas gauge needle as it sank lower and lower toward the small black mark that signified empty.

TWELVE

The worst happened.

Five miles short of the NATO military base and airstrip, the engine of the Land-Rover coughed, spat, rattled, and died.

"Goddamn it!" Nick Carter cursed as he hit the steering wheel with the heels of his hands.

Even if the tank had been filled to the brim as the rental agency had promised, he knew that for every mile the vehicle traveled through the heavy snow, zigzagging around stalled cars and trucks and motorcycles, the wheels had been spinning from two to three miles.

Carter calculated how long it would take him to walk to the base. The storm had, if possible, intensified, and he was lucky to see the white mounds of stalled vehicles on the highway ahead. The headlights of the Land-Rover still shone brightly, illuminating the myriad tumbling, glistening snowflakes.

Even if he could make it through this blizzard, it would take hours. He would be heading directly into the wind, into the teeth of the storm.

He refused to concede that Raina Missou, Minya Stalin, and Julio Vasco had won. At dawn tomorrow, less than twelve hours away, Neil Steiner, no doubt frightened sick for the safety of his family, would do his job as ordered. He'd tap in, avert the thwarting devices, and fire the cruise missile at a remote Russian target.

The cruise missile, Carter knew, was a marvel of technological sophistication. It was a weapon unaffected by storms. It had interior defenses against exterior forces. It would cut through the blizzard like a hot knife through butter. The Soviets would pick it up on radar, give a brief warning, and then, as their antiballistic missile system went into effect, they would barrage the West with a volley of propaganda, followed quite possibly by short- and long-range missiles in sufficient volume to make World War IV an impossibility.

He looked gloomily out at the storm through the windshield. There was no way to hitch a ride. Except for the occasional snowmobile, nothing was moving out there but wind and snow. And he hadn't seen a snowmobile for the last few minutes.

Out of frustration, he pressed on the horn button and kept on pressing, barely hearing the blare of it above the howling wind.

Carter knew that the sound of the horn probably did not travel more than ten feet from the Land-Rover, but at least he was doing something while he was thinking. He would keep honking until the horn broke or until the battery died from pure exhaustion.

He began to feel the cold creep into the vehicle, through invisible cracks that apparently were everywhere. In an hour, perhaps even sooner, it would be freezing cold inside the car. He pulled the knit ski hat further down over his ears.

Should he stay and freeze in the car, or should he strike out for the base and freeze on the highway?

"Some choice," he muttered above the blaring of the horn. "Some lovely choice."

The man from AXE did not have a monopoly on frustration. In the cozy, warm little hotel beside the wharf in Copenhagen, Minya Stalin had lost all patience with the blond, blue-eyed Danish captain who refused, despite the trio's ministrations, to sober up.

"We must leave within two hours," he said, "or we will miss the warship altogether. We must find another captain and another ship that can make it to Rügen through this storm. The storm isn't going to cease, as this drunken sot kept promising, so we go in spite of it."

"I agree that Captain Norrstrom has been a disappointment," Raina Missou said with a slow nod of her lovely head, "but I tried every boat up and down the wharves. This man is the only one foolish enough, or who has the proper ship, to even attempt a crossing in this weather."

Raina, Stalin, and Vasco were sitting in one of the rooms. On the floor, quietly singing some Danish sea song, was Captain Lars Norrstrom. He was smiling, occasionally laughing to himself, but standing, or even sitting in a chair, was beyond his present capabilities. The drugs were keeping him awake, but it seemed that the only way the captain could sober up would be if he were allowed to sleep off those quarts of wine. And waiting that long was out of the question.

"We will find another captain and another ship," Stalin said, rising and staring disgustedly at the man sprawled on the floor.

"Do you mind telling us just how you will perform this miraculous feat?" General Vasco asked, fingering the hideous scar just beneath his white beard.

"We shall pool our financial resources," Minya Stalin announced. "Between us, we should have many thousands of dollars. We offer all of it as a reward for the captain who gets us to Rügen."

Raina and the Cuban general considered the plan, and since they were prepared to do practically anything in the world for enough money, they figured that everybody else was, too. The Russian's idea made sense to them. Both men pulled billfolds from inside breast pockets, and Raina grabbed her purse. They emptied their contents onto a bed, and Stalin slowly counted it.

"Well?" Raina said anxiously as he finished his count and continued to study the pile of money. "How much do we have?"

"Unbelievable," the KGB man said. "How could we carry so much money all through Tangier and escape the famous pickpockets there? And in Paris as well."

"How much, *amigo?*" General Vasco demanded.

"We have just over a hundred thousand dollars in cash," Minya Stalin replied. "With that much money, we can buy the Danish navy and all the men in it."

"True," Raina said, "but no amount of money is going to change the weather."

THE ASSASSIN CONVENTION

"Let us go downstairs and spread the word," General Vasco said somewhat officiously. "My guess is that we will be at sea within the hour. For enough money, some other captain may decide it's worth it to be a little crazy."

The man on the snowmobile saw the dimming headlights and heard the muted blaring of the horn. His name was François Bruggeman, and he was a member of the French National Rescue Patrol. He had a huge plastic hamper of provisions in a special compartment behind his seat. So far that day he had helped fifty stranded motorists and their families.

Bruggeman smiled because he was now about to add to his list of rescues and gain immense credit from his duty commander when he returned to headquarters.

He eased back on the hand throttle and brought the snowmobile up alongside the red Land-Rover with the dim headlights and softly blaring horn. He wiped snow from the window and saw that the man inside was alone. There were no children to save. That was a disappointment; children always brought special credit to the members of the patrol.

The man inside the Land-Rover looked dead to Bruggeman. His head had dropped forward to the steering wheel, and the weight of that head was depressing the horn button. *Mon Dieu*, Bruggeman thought, *the poor wretch must be dead*. There were no credits given for reporting the dead; it was merely another statistic to be filed and forgotten.

Ice had formed on the man's lips and around his nose and eyes. His eyebrows were encrusted with ice. Why had he shut down his engine and left his lights on? Bruggeman wondered, then realized the Land-Rover must be out of gas, but the battery had enough life to keep the lights and horn going.

Bruggeman shut off the engine of the snowmobile and slowly dismounted. His slow movements were dictated by the force of the wind, the intensity of the cold, and the thickness of his cold-weather gear. He was also a little stiff from the hours he had spent straddling the machine and rumbling over mostly rough terrain. He opened the door of the Land-Rover and reached in to check the driver's pulse, at the neck.

A hand gripped his wrist, a hand with the strength of steel.

"What is this?" Bruggeman bellowed. "It is all right, *monsieur*. I am only trying to help you."

"Who are you?" Nick Carter demanded. He still kept his grip on the man's wrist.

Bruggeman explained that he was the senior member of the National Rescue Patrol and that he had seen the headlights and heard the horn and had stopped to see if he could be of help and had thought the man behind the wheel was dead and . . . Carter had to interrupt to shut him off.

"Can you get me to the NATO military base near here?" he demanded.

"My instructions, *monsieur*, are to provide blankets and provisions, and to give advice," Bruggeman replied. "I am afraid that I cannot take you anywhere. I shall report your request to my duty commander, and he will have someone sent out to fetch you."

Carter tried to keep his temper in check. He knew about men like François Bruggeman. They were good men, but they were like robots programmed to do a certain job and never to deviate from the narrow line of their assigned duties. Faithfulness to instructions—to the very letter—was their watchword.

The man from AXE wiped snow and ice from his face. He looked at the patrolman and at the snowmobile, then took a deep breath of frigid air.

"I don't have time to explain everything," he said, his voice as calm and deliberate as he could make it. He was already late and didn't want to waste a word. And every word he did say had to make a profound impression on this well-meaning man.

"Listen to me very carefully, *mon ami*. I am an agent of the United States government on a very delicate mission. The lives of millions of people depend on my getting to that NATO air base as soon as possible. I need your snowmobile and your cooperation. You look like a reasonable man, but I am warning you: I will be on that machine of yours with or without your cooperation. And," Carter added, knowing that men like Bruggeman thrive on brownie points from their superiors, "when this is all over, I will make certain that the President of the United States sends a personal commendation to your government citing your assistance in avoiding what may have been an international crisis with terrible consequences and many, many dead."

Bruggeman looked at him, his mouth open.

"When we get to the NATO base, the personnel there will vouch for my identity. This is not some outlandish fairy tale, *monsieur*. I am telling you the truth. Well?"

The promise of a governmental citation, plus Carter's

unyielding grip on his wrist, convinced Bruggeman that cooperation was the order of the day. Blankets and provisions to stranded motorists would have to wait.

"All right," Bruggeman said, smiling and puffing out his chest as he thought of such an honor on his record. "Come. I will help you onto the seat behind me. We shall be at the base in a few minutes and I shall be back saving snowbound travelers a few minutes after that. Let's go!"

A minute later, Carter was on the back of the seat, clinging to the back of his rescuer. He shivered as the demonic gusts of wind blew at them across the open field.

Bruggeman turned the key in the ignition, and the engine burst into life. The snowmobile shot off down the cluttered highway, zigzagging around stalled vehicles that looked like little white igloos as the snow piled up around them. The wind was howling like a clutch of banshees gathered for a witch's wake.

In spite of the cold, in spite of his personal discomfort and the almost unbearable tension of the situation, Nick Carter had trouble keeping awake as he hung onto the back of the man who had saved his life, and quite possibly the whole world.

But, as the poem said, Carter noted, there were miles to go before he slept. The deadly trio were miles and hours ahead of him. Storm or no storm, they were dedicated to their own evil cause and would find a way to effect their plan. They were as determined to succeed in their scheme as he was to stop them.

François Bruggeman turned out to be a master at the controls of the snowmobile. He had Carter at the base in the few minutes he promised, and though Carter felt awful physically, his spirits revived, and he was grateful to the man. NATO guards, checking Carter's special identification and knowing that he was to arrive, waved the two men through the gates. Bruggeman was impressed.

And then the roof caved in on Nick Carter.

The jet that had been readied by a special on-base crew had been shut down. A tractor called a "mule" was pulling the military plane back to the safety of an enormous hangar.

"Sorry," the pilot told Nick Carter. "We waited until the snow was so thick on the wings that it would have taken a snowblower to get it off. The base commander ordered the shutdown, and he's the only one who can order another startup. Just between you and me, sir, he's pissed to the max about this whole thing. Thought I'd warn you."

"I don't give a damn about his feelings," Carter said to the startled young pilot as the plane was being ushered back into its lair. "Where can I find the base commander?"

The pilot shook his head as if to say that Carter really was a glutton for punishment. "He's at home," he said. And he gave Carter directions to the man's home.

Carter turned to seek out his rescuer, hoping to talk the man into taking him to the home of the base commander.

But François Bruggeman was gone. Having delivered Carter to the base and seeing him talking to the pilot, he'd decided his job was done. He'd remounted his snowmobile and was on his way back to his job of rescuing stranded motorists.

Leaving Carter to rescue a stranded planet.

In Copenhagen, luck was much better for the trio of

conspirators. They were proceeding only a bit behind schedule on their plan to lob that cruise missile into Russia.

They had found a captain who, for a hundred thousand dollars, would try to swim to Rügen with the three foreigners on his back. The captain's name was Nils Bridevell. Though his boat was smaller than the one owned by Norrstrom, it was a tough little sea warrior and, as Captain Bridevell told them, had been out in much worse storms. And there was one gigantic plus: Captain Nils Bridevell was stone cold sober when he agreed to take them. His decision to ferry Raina Missou, Minya Stalin, and General Julio Vasco to the waiting Polish warship off the coast of East Germany, near the island of Rügen, was made while drunk with the idea of what a hundred thousand American dollars in tax-free cash would do for his future as a fisherman.

Captain Bridevell had even helped carry the now sleeping hulk of his competitor, Lars Norrstrom, down to a dim corner of the hotel's bar where he could sleep off his enormous intake of glög. Bridevell and his three new employers sat in one of the upstairs rooms, plotting the voyage to Rügen.

"I have sent notice to my crew," the efficient captain was saying. "They will be aboard the *Hanseatic Queen* in less than thirty minutes. The engines will require a ten-minute warm-up period, and after clearance from the Port Authority chief—another ten-minute task—we shall be on our way to Rügen." The captain held up his hands to ward off protests from the three who had hired him at such a stunning fee. "I know, you would like to leave immediately, but that is impossible."

"And why is that?" Minya Stalin demanded.

"Because of the storm," Captain Bridevell explained patiently, "we must take all precautionary measures. The crew cannot be on board in less than thirty minutes. Without a ten-minute warm-up of the engines, we would stall at sea, in which case we would founder and sink. Without clearance from authorities, I would never dare take my boat out of this port during a storm. Be patient. In one hour we shall be on a direct heading for Rügen, all engines full. Trust me."

"All right," Raina said, answering for all of them. "We trust you, but can we trust your boat? Will it make it through this storm?"

"Madame," the captain said, drawing himself up and looking offended, "you will not insult my boat. The *Hanseatic Queen* and its captain know tricks of the sea that remain mysteries to that drunken lout named Lars Norrstrom and his battered old tugboat, the *Little Mermaid*. To show you my faith in myself and my vessel, I will not accept a single dollar of your generous fee until after I have delivered you to your destination."

"Yes," said General Vasco as he stroked his throat and the scar there, "and supposing we decided at some point to throw you overboard and keep our money."

The captain smiled.

"In which case," he said confidently, "you would sink and die. As I said, both my vessel and I know certain tricks and mysteries of the sea. Without me, your entire venture is useless."

The Cuban general, however, was thinking of the moment when the Polish warship picked them up off the coast of Rügen. The captain guessed his thoughts.

"For your information," he said, "many of our fishing boats are equipped with a single torpedo and tube to be used to fight off Soviet fishing boats that encroach upon our waters. If anything happens to me at the moment you are transferred from my boat to the Polish warship, my men will have instructions to fire the torpedo at close range. If a double cross is in your minds, my friends, I would advise you to purge such a thought. Do we have an agreement?"

"We have," Minya Stalin said. He was the first one to shake the hand of the small but powerfully built Danish captain; it was a gesture of respect for a man who, like Stalin, thought of everything and was quite capable of destroying himself and those around him if he were in any way betrayed. Stalin liked the captain, but his mind still toyed with the idea of betrayal if he could think of a way to do it without getting himself killed in the process.

A hundred thousand dollars was a lot of money to an aging KGB man who wanted to retire to a *dacha* on the Black Sea.

THIRTEEN

Lt. General Doyle Peck, commander of the NATO air base near the Belgian border, was in a foul mood.

The blizzard had made his normal job difficult enough without having to take orders from some Pentagon bigshot and readying a jet to get some special agent to Denmark. He didn't want his plane and men out in this mess. Not unless it was absolutely necessary. Like because of a war, perhaps.

But he'd done it. And then the guy didn't show up. He had a few million dollars' worth of hardware to protect, and a few tons of snow settling on the wings as it sat on the runway didn't help things any. He was glad he'd cancelled the whole business. He reached for the bottle of red wine and refilled his wife's and then his own glass.

Elizabeth Peck tried to salvage what had turned out to be—between the weather and her husband—a very bad day by lighting a fire in the fireplace and preparing a special dinner. In spite of her attempts to create a cheerful atmosphere, her husband had hardly said a word since they'd sat down to dinner.

She nearly dropped her fork when the telephone rang. She glanced at her husband, who looked even more annoyed at the intrusion, then got up to answer it.

"Hello?" she answered, then listened, and after a few moments she covered the mouthpiece with her hand. "Doyle, it's for you. A man says he must talk to you. He says it's very important."

"Who is it?" the general asked, chewing. He heard his wife ask the caller for his identity.

"He won't tell me. He'll only talk to you, and he says it's about the jet."

Peck put down his knife and fork. "Elizabeth, tell whoever it is that unless he tells you his name, he might as well hang up."

She told the caller that the general insisted upon knowing who was calling. Then there was the sound of the receiver being replaced in its cradle.

Elizabeth Peck returned to her seat at the table. "He wouldn't say his name on the phone. He said it was too dangerous on an open line."

Peck lifted an eyebrow, glanced at his wife, then returned to his dinner. "Open line?" He shook his head. "Are you aware of how many nuisance calls we get from people who want to play spy? This is a NATO air base. It's no secret. We have hangars full of jets. Why couldn't this guy tell me what was so important? A lot of people read too many international thrillers, and being snowbound sends them all to the telephone." He took a sip of wine. "I must reprimand the switchboard about giving out my private number," he muttered as he stabbed a piece of steak.

"Yes, dear," said Elizabeth Peck.

Nick Carter didn't waste any time.

Immediately after hanging up, he dialed Hawk's special number with the built-in scrambler and waited for AXE's director to come on the line. The arrogance of some military brass had to be experienced to be believed. Wouldn't the fact that he'd called on the base commander's private line at home have made some impression? Carter wondered. Hadn't the general been given minimal details about the reason behind Washington's unorthodox request for transportation? Carter was shaking his head in disgust when Hawk's gravelly voice said, "What's going on, N3? Where are you?"

Carter told him about what happened—or rather what *hadn't* happened—at the NATO air base and of his fruitless attempt to reach the general. Not having a scrambler device with him, he wasn't going to try to explain the urgency of his situation by detailing the mission for the entire world to hear over an open line.

"I know I was late, sir, but it couldn't be helped." He gave Hawk a quick rundown of his detour to rescue the Steiners. "And the weather here is beyond belief. It's become worse, if possible. The three in Copenhagen can't fly in this white-out to the lighthouse, so they'll have to go by boat—if they can find a skipper crazy enough to go out in this storm. My theory is that if I can stop them in

Copenhagen, there will be no need to enter Soviet-bloc waters. I won't need that ship I asked for.''

"It's a good thing," Hawk said, "because we were turned down on the boat. The Navy's not risking men and a boat in this storm. Do you really think they're still in Denmark?''

"Yes, sir, I do.''

"All right. We'll put some pressure on this General Peck from here and see how he might like being commandant of a remote desk in the Pentagon. Give me twenty minutes and call him again.''

"If you don't mind, sir,'' Carter said, "I'd prefer that you have the general call me at the operations shed at the base. It's not that I want to humiliate him, but at this point every minute is precious.''

"I can understand that. Just hold tight.''

Ten minutes later, after a few brief words between Carter and a now very contrite general, the chief of operations was put on the line, and when he was finished, snowblowers were dispatched to clean the snow off the wings of the jet and a mule tractor hauled it out of the hangar.

In minutes, the Killmaster was airborne in the sleek silver plane en route to Copenhagen.

The pilot had nerves of steel, and they made good time despite the turbulence. The landing was rough because the pilot chose not to use a previously cleared strip. Most of the runways were open, thanks to plows and graders and half-tracks, but the wind had shifted at the last minute, and to avoid a crosswind, the pilot decided to land on an uncleared runway.

THE ASSASSIN CONVENTION

Soon after landing, a hopeful Nick Carter was on his way to see the commandant of the base.

At the very moment Carter's plane touched down at the snow-covered military base north of Copenhagen, the *Hanseatic Queen* was casting off its lines in the churning harbor. Captain Nils Bridevell, at the wheel, gave crisp orders to his sailors. All went well.

The boat, built for fishing in the stormy North Atlantic or the equally stormy Baltic, plowed smoothly through the choppy waves in the harbor, then met a series of walls of water in the open sea.

The engines labored, the propellors squealed in protest, the sailors cursed, the captain set his jaw grimly, and the *Hanseatic Queen*—its decks and rigging encrusted with frosty white ice decorations—moved slowly away from land.

The boat slowed from eight knots in the harbor to a laboring three knots in the open sea. There were times, the captain, crew, and three passengers were convinced, when it seemed as if the ship made no headway at all and was at the mercy of the waves in the storm-tossed seas.

Below in their cabins, Raina Missou, Minya Stalin, and General Julio Vasco lay on their bunks and clung to anything that didn't move under their grip. They could not stand or walk in the cabins without danger of being slammed brutally against the bulkheads.

Five minutes after clearing the relative protection of the harbor, Raina Missou became violently sick. A few minutes after that, Minya Stalin followed suit. General Vasco, whose Latin machismo wouldn't let him admit to seasickness, lay on his bunk and turned an interesting shade of green beneath his white beard before he, too, lurched into the head.

A half hour after leaving port, Captain Nils Bridevell knew that the *Hanseatic Queen* had gone only five miles from shore. At this rate, the fishing boat would never reach Rügen in time to meet the Polish warship.

Many times, the captain considered turning back. If the storm worsened, for example, the boat could easily be sunk. At the very best, they would miss the warship and the voyage would have been for nothing. He was certain that his paying passengers were quite capable, in that event, to toss him overboard once they were certain that they could handle the crew themselves.

But the lure of a hundred thousand dollars, and the thought of how many fishing boats he could buy with that much money, kept him on course. Even though he could not see where he was going, the magnetic compass in its lighted binnacle told him all he needed to know.

Yawing and pitching notwithstanding, the bobbing little boat was on a heading for Rügen Island.

And Captain Nils Bridevell would reach that island before midnight, or he would die in the effort.

"Please don't force me to make a call to Washington," Nick Carter told the commandant of the NATO facility in Denmark. "The last call produced results for me but almost got a transfer for General Peck to a Pentagon desk."

"But what you ask is impossible," the base commander told him. "All our jeeps are stuck in this wet snow. The only vehicles that can get through are half-tracks. We

146

have six of them, and they're all busy clearing runways.''

''Do the job with five,'' Carter said. ''I need one to get me into the city, preferably the wharves. I don't need another plane, General Westfield, I need a boat.''

''In this storm?'' the general replied, laughing. ''You won't find a boat seaworthy enough to make it out of the harbor, much less a captain crazy enough to try.''

''All the better,'' Carter said, grinning. ''If I can't find one, the people I'm looking for can't find one. The point is, I know they're down there trying, and I have to stop them before they succeed. If they do succeed, I have to find a way to beat them to their destination. Now, General Westfield, about that half-track . . .''

''Impossible,'' the general repeated. ''For one thing, our half-tracks aren't licensed to travel on . . .''

Carter started to reach for the telephone on the desk. His eyes never left the general's.

''All right.'' Westfield sighed. ''You can have one half-track and one driver. But I want them back here within the hour or I make my *own* call to Washington.''

Carter stood up. He offered his right hand and managed a smile. ''You'll have them back, sir. And thank you for your cooperation.''

General Westfield shook Carter's hand but didn't return the smile. ''If that machine isn't back in an hour, I'll have your ass, Carter.''

''No disrespect intended, General Westfield,'' Carter said wryly, ''but you'll have to stand in line for that.''

The big half-track made the trip to the city easily. Carter could hardly believe that the vehicle didn't even shudder from the high snowdrifts or driving winds.

As he rumbled into Copenhagen with a young, rugged airman at the controls, Carter settled back and thought. He hoped he would find Raina Missou, Minya Stalin, and General Julio Vasco still in the city, trying to con a fisherman into taking them across the sea in his boat. It would not be easy facing down such a gathering, but it was preferable to having to find a boat and crossing that strip of churning water to the Polish coast.

And then it occurred to him that even if he met and killed the three principals in the scheme, he would still have to get to that lighthouse.

A man named Neil Steiner was there with the proper codes to tap into NATO's computers and to fire off a cruise missile. Steiner would carry out the mission because he believed that his wife and three children were being held hostage. And Steiner would undoubtedly be surrounded by armed men to make certain that no one interfered with the task. Although Carter was fairly sure that the missile wouldn't be fired until Stalin, Raina Missou, and Genral Vasco got to the lighthouse, he couldn't be absolutely certain.

"How are we doing?" Carter asked the young man driving the half-track.

"The city's just ahead," the airman replied. "I'll have you at the docks in ten minutes. That time enough?"

"It had better be," Carter said, almost to himself. "It just better be."

Out in the Baltic, the storm had eased. The wind dropped to near normal and the snow fell in soft drops. The waves that had come close to pounding the bow off the *Hanseatic Queen* and turned to great swells that rode the boat upward and onward. Captain Nils Bridevell could see past the bow for the first time, but there was nothing out there but the blackness of the frigid night.

The captain was smiling as he gazed down at the compass. He winked at his first mate, who stood in the little wheelhouse beside him.

"Right on target, Erik," he said. "I couldn't have done better if the seas had been calm. Have you checked on our well-paying passengers?"

"Just did, Captain," the first mate said. "The cabins are a mess. All three of them are very seasick."

The captain continued to smile, thinking, *Let them make all the mess they want, just as long as they don't do anything to ruin that hundred thousand dollars*. But he said, "They will be fine shortly. With the letup in the storm, we'll have smooth sailing and arrive at Rügen in"—he looked at his wristwatch—"less than three hours, well under our time limit."

"I believe it, Captain," the first mate said, smiling back at the tough-looking skipper who had made the deal of a lifetime, although he didn't know exactly how much was involved.

"And I won't forget you and the crew," Captain Bridevell said generously. "A two-thousand-dollar bonus for you, Erik, and a thousand apiece for the others."

"Very good, sir," the first mate said appreciatively. He didn't think of two thousand dollars as a pittance for having risked his life; he couldn't make that much money on twenty runs to Rügen and back. His wife would be so happy when he got home and told her about his unexpected windfall. "May I go tell the others of this good fortune?"

"Certainly." Captain Bridevell wanted his generosity to be known. "And while you're down below, have the crew clean the cabins and change the bedding. We must make our passengers as comfortable as possible."

When Erik left the bridge, both he and the captain were singing, happy, as the Danish saying goes, as a reindeer on ice.

The storm hadn't yet left the land.

Nick Carter bent into the wind after the half-track's young driver had let him off where the Grand Canal empties into the harbor. The young soldier had said cheerfully, "Well, here we are, sir, the Paris of the north."

Some Paris, Carter thought gloomily as he gazed through the pelting snow and biting wind at the murky waterfront. Then again, he realized, any city in a storm would be uninviting. Even Paris itself had been pretty bleak once the storm had begun in earnest.

Copenhagen was indeed called the Paris of the north. It was, under less inclement conditions, a very beautiful city, Carter had to admit. It was not only the largest city in Scandinavia, it was the most important seaport and commercial fishing center on the Baltic.

Carter had been to Copenhagen many times, and he had enjoyed prowling the old city and the new, taking boat rides on the many canals, walking through Tivoli Gardens, and drinking and dining at the uncountable sidewalk cafes. And he had always found Danish women very attractive.

Right now, though, Carter decided he would enjoy being warm. He made a beeline for the first glow of light, and was ushered into a warm tavern on a gust of wind and snow. It was a cheerful place. The people there considered themselves stranded by the storm and were making the most of it. Most of the customers, Carter noted, were feeling no pain.

Carter had a drink and a cigarette, and stayed just long enough to learn that the bartender, who was reasonably sober, had not seen Raina Missou and her two escorts. Reluctantly, he left the rowdy, friendly company and went out to battle the storm.

He worked that whole side of the street, going from the Grand Canal to Havn Street. His body was protesting the radical changes from bitter cold to steamy warmth. He felt like someone being tortured by being placed in a steam bath and then hauled out periodically to be thrown into an icy swimming pool.

And then he noticed that there was one more glowing sign three buildings past Havn Street. He walked into the howling wind and blinding snow to that sign and saw that it was a small hotel. It wasn't one of Copenhagen's finest, but it wasn't one of its worst, either. Carter went inside.

There was a tiny lobby in front. At the rear, up two wide, carpeted steps, was a restaurant and bar. A few noisy customers were laughing and drinking at the tables; a few more were sleeping it off with glasses, steins, and even bottles still in their hands.

He checked out the staircase leading to rooms upstairs and knew that he had to be in the right place because he had tried all the others. Carter was convinced that Raina, Stalin, and Vasco would stay at a dockside hotel. There was no way they could fly tonight, so a boat was the only answer. He was equally certain that even among these fun- and drink-loving Danes, they hadn't found a skipper drunk enough or crazy enough to venture out to sea on such a night.

Carter approached the hotel's desk.

"Hey, mister, what can I do for you?" the clerk asked jovially. He too had been sampling the bar's stock to keep in the spirit of the storm and of being stranded. "Do you want a room for the night?"

"Maybe," Carter said. "First, some information."

To speed things along, he put two bills on the counter. They were hundred-dollar bills. The clerk's eyes stared at the money.

"This is for me?" he asked hopefully. "For what?"

"For information," Carter replied. He described Raina Missou, Minya Stalin, and General Vasco to the clerk, as he had to hotel clerks all down the street.

"They were here," the clerk said, his eyes never leaving the two bills on the counter. Just to make certain the man was well hooked, Carter added a fifty-dollar bill. "But those names are unfamiliar to me. Two rooms on the third floor were rented by the man with the hard blue eyes, but his name is Andrei Stanislav, not Minya Stalin."

Carter added another fifty. He had hit pay dirt. "Are they still in their rooms?" he asked.

The clerk shook his head. "Nope, I'm afraid they left almost an hour ago. They left, hard as it may be to believe, on a fishing boat named the *Hanseatic Queen*, captained by Nils Bridevell. I don't know when they were going, but they were in a reall hurry to get moving. I'll bet they're at

152

the bottom of the ocean by now.''

"No such luck,'' Carter said under his breath, but the clerk didn't hear him. "May I go up to see their rooms?'' Carter asked. "Maybe they left something that could tell me their destination.''

"You'd be wasting your time,'' the clerk said. "My wife has already cleaned both rooms and changed the linen. The rooms were hardly used. You can have the rooms if you like, mister, no charge. Your friends paid for the week, so—''

"Thank you,'' Carter said, suddenly feeling tired and defeated. "I'll take one of the rooms if I need it. But tell me something. If they could find a skipper to take them out on a night like this, he must be one hell of a seaman. And if there is one top-notch sailor in Copenhagen, there must be others. Do you know of any I could approach?''

The clerk glanced toward tthe bar, as though to make certain they weren't being heard. Carter shared the glance and turned back to face the clerk. He noticed that the money was now gone.

"Before your friends located Captain Bridevell and the *Hanseatic Queen*,'' he said, "they spent a lot of time with a far better seaman who owns a far better and faster boat.''

Carter's hopes soared again. He felt like a gambler who hit the jackpot just often enough to make it all worthwhile, sometimes making his strike on his last dollar. "Who is this man?'' he asked. "Where can I find him?''

The clerk jerked a thumb toward the bar. "His name is Lars Norrstrom, and his boat is named the *Little Mermaid*. He's at a table near the back of the bar, smashed. That's his big problem. Booze. Your friends found him but couldn't keep him sober enough to make the journey. That is why they left him here and went with Captain Bridevell.''

Carter grinned and put another hundred-dollar bill on the counter.

''I'll sober him up and find out if my friends are dead or alive. Point him out to me.''

The clerk shook his head, letting Carter know that he wouldn't be so optimistic, but he took him to where Captain Lars Norrstrom sat, head on the table, snoring loudly. The big Dane had a glass of dark red wine clutched in a fist.

The hope that had once again begun to rush through Carter's veins slowed and stopped as he stared at the sleeping man. It was not going to be easy to get Captain Norrstrom to cooperate.

FOURTEEN

Nick Carter sat down at the table where Captain Norrstrom slept. He put a hand on the big Dane's shoulder and started shaking him, all the while repeating his name.

Norrstrom finally opened a bloodshot eye. His head was on its side on the table.

"I want some information and I need to use your boat," he heard a voice say.

"Go away," the captain growled. "I'm asleep." The red-veined eye closed.

"I'm willing to pay you very well if you cooperate. If you don't cooperate, you're going to be killed by 'dockside hoodlums' after you eventually leave this bar."

The eye snapped open this time. It found itself staring into the muzzle of a 9mm Luger that rested on the table's edge. Carter's coat kept it hidden from other eyes in the bar.

In his long career, Carter had discovered that the adrenaline generated by mortal fear was often a better cure for a hangover than any number of cold showers and quarts of coffee.

"What the hell . . ." the blond man said as he sat up with a start, the glass in his hand tipping over and spilling wine on the floor.

"I don't have much time, Captain Norrstrom. I'm in great need of your services." Carter held Wilhelmina in his right hand, and in his left he produced a roll of bills. "There's a lot more to come, Captain, if you help me. I'd much rather pay you than kill you."

"I'm listening."

"Point Lochsa, twenty miles northeast of Gdynia, Poland," Carter said. "There's a lighthouse there I have to check out."

Captain Norrstrom scratched his head and gazed at Carter with a perplexed look. He seemed to be putting bits and pieces together in his mind, things he'd been told and things he'd overheard while drunk. It was a long minute before he spoke.

"Mister, if you want to find your three friends, you go where they went, not to some lighthouse in Poland."

"Would you repeat that, please?" Carter asked. "Or explain it?"

"Simple," Lars Norrstrom said, fingering the roll of bills on the table. "Your friends wanted to go to the island of Rügen, off the East German coast. There, they were to meet a Polish warship that would take them—well, they did not say. So, my friend, you wish to go to Rügen, not to Poland."

At last Carter had some solid information. He felt the

big Dane was telling him what he knew. The whole plan was obvious: the three would enter Polish waters on a Polish warship so they would not be stopped. How they had arranged that, Carter had no idea, but he had to admit it was a smart move. He guessed it was probably Minya Stalin's doing. Considering the weather, another question gnawed at Carter's mind. Why were they all risking their lives to reach the lighthouse? Steiner was there, supposedly ready if not exactly willing to do what he had to. Did only Stalin—or Raina or even Vasco—have data necessary to complete the computer entry that would launch the cruise missile? Did the trio make itself the indispensible final link in the chain?

A map of the area suddenly appeared in Carter's mind, etched on his fine memory. It was a long way from Copenhagen to Rügen, but it was even farther from there to Point Lochsa. But if a boat left Copenhagen on a direct line to the lighthouse . . . . Even with the head start, the three conspirators still might not reach the lighthouse until after Carter's arrival.

It was a gamble, but in the life of a Killmaster for AXE, nearly everything was a gamble.

"Come on," he said to the Dane. "Let's go to your boat."

"In an hour," Captain Norrstrom said defiantly. "In an hour, the storm will—"

"Now," Carter said quietly as he raised the muzzle of the Luger so the Danish captain could see the whole gun. He also slammed his left hand down on the money. "You want the money and your life. You'll keep both if you do what I say."

Ten minutes later, they were aboard the *Little Mermaid*, with only the captain and Carter as crew. But the boat with the powerful diesel engines did not require a large crew. Lars Norrstrom was all business as he fired up the powerful engines and eased out of the berth and into the habor. The hotel clerk was correct in his assessment of the seaman's abilities. Carter, who had cast off the lines, was quickly on the bridge to make certain the waves in the harbor didn't push them into a piling.

The storm had abated by the time they reached the end of the seawall that formed the great harbor.

"See?" Captain Norrstrom said, taking credit for the change in the weather. "I've been saying all along that it would cease in an hour. I kept telling your friends that. I was right."

"Sure," Carter said. *Keep predicting something long enough and eventually you'll hit it on the nose*. "Captain, give her full throttle and set her on a heading for Point Lochsa."

The man from AXE studied the map and watched the compass to make certain that his orders were followed. They were headed in a southeasterly direction and making good time. When the *Little Mermaid* was chugging through the high swells directly toward the lighthouse many miles away, he relaxed—a little.

But halfway across the long stretch of water between Copenhagen and Point Lochsa, the storm rose with new fury, and the tough little boat found it slow going. Captain Norrstrom, taking the bad weather as a personal insult, cursed the storm and the engines and the gods and, most of all, the man who had wakened him from his stupor and, with a gun aimed at his gut, had convinced him this trip would be a good idea.

Carter, sensing the man's anger and knowing that some of it was caused by his hangover, knew that another part had to do with money. He had no idea what the trio had offered him or were paying the other captain, Nils Bridevell. He thought quickly and, considering the risk factors of the weather and the fact that they would be entering enemy waters, came up with a figure.

"I'm sorry I had to use the gun to get you to do this," he said as he stood beside the captain and watched the heaving of the bow as the storm worsened. "We never got around to mentioning a final figure. I don't have the cash with me, but I can guarantee you that shortly after our return, you'll have in your hands twenty-five thousand American dollars."

Captain Lars Norrstrom grinned and nodded. That crazy woman with the golden skin and that Russian with the sharp eyes and that stupid general with the white beard and heavy Spanish accent had offered only ten thousand. He was pleased. Now, if he only had a drink, or if the lousy hangover would just let up—not to mention the storm he had thought was over—things would be perfect. But a part of his mind was already figuring what one hell of a time he would have with that twenty-five thousand dollars. The night was turning out well.

Four miles northwest of the island of Rügen, the Polish destroyer moved with difficulty through the choppy waves. The captain had ordered the bow into the wind when the storm returned with a vengeance, and though he

was to pick up his friend Andrei Stanislav and his friends
on the fishing boat nearer the island, he had to head out to
sea a bit because of the storm. It was not quite eleven
o'clock, and there was ample time before he would have
to depart for good, but he was worried.

The storm had let up for a short time, and that was a
good sign. Even though snow still fell heavily, he knew
that his bright searchlights would be seen by Andrei, and
that his own lookouts would spot their boat once it came
relatively near. What worried the skipper of the destroyer
was not the chance missing of Andrei and his friends, it
was the radio message he had received thirty minutes ago:

SMALL CRAFT FROM VICINITY OF DENMARK LOCATED ON
RADAR AT 55 DEGREES LATITUDE AND 18 DEGREES LON-
GITUDE, ON HEADING FOR POINT LOCHSA. IF CRAFT CONTIN-
UES ON PRESENT COURSE, INTERCEPT AND TURN BACK. FIRE
IF NECESSARY.

And only a minute ago, a second message had come,
ordering the destroyer to intercept the small craft because
it was nearing Polish waters. If he left immediately, he
would be able to comply with the orders; if he delayed, the
craft would slip through. There were no other Polish ships
at sea; none was large enough to survive this storm—none
but the one beneath the captain's feet.

What made the skipper of the destroyer hesitate in
obeying orders was another coded message that told him
that yet another small craft was entering East German
waters from Denmark. The Polish captain knew that this
second craft contained his friend Andrei. As for the craft

headed for the same eventual destination as Andrei, yet in a more direct routing, the skipper had no idea what it was or why it was playing such a dangerous game.

All the Polish captain knew for certain was that, friendship or no friendship, he would give Andrei Stanislav and his associates five more minutes of his precious time, then he would set out after the craft that was already on the way to Point Lochsa. Orders were orders.

The skipper ordered the huge ship about and started a downwind run. But the renewed intensity of the storm made him wonder if he were making the right decision.

At the lighthouse on Point Lochsa, Neil Steiner sat at a computer terminal and watched with interest as a mock war was played out by bored NATO computer operators. The computer war game consisted of sending every Allied missile in existence into the heart of Russia. For realism, the NATO screen jockeys had the Soviets fire all their antiballistic and then all their tactical and intercontinental projectiles at the heart of America. The Americans then fired their own antiballistic missiles and the screen was jammed with simulated explosion after explosion.

And then the screen cleared when Steiner tired of watching the game and punched the proper buttons.

"Why'd you do that?" the man behind him groused. "It was just gettin' interestin'."

"I have to send a message," Steiner told the two armed men who were his constant and unwanted companions.

"What message?" the second man demanded, suspicious.

"Never mind," Steiner said. He'd had enough bullying

from the goons left to guard him. Four clones of these two were down below, watching the black night for a sign of the Polish warship bearing the KGB man, the Morrocan woman, and the Cuban general. "You wouldn't understand it anyway," Steiner added.

The computer expert who had stolen NATO's code for tapping into the cruise missile controls—all the code but the digits kept by the KGB man—quickly tapped into a *Sûreté* terminal in that police organization's Paris headquarters. He had been sending a cryptic message to them hourly since he had arrived at the lighthouse. So far, nothing had come of it. But he had to keep trying.

"Oh, I get it," the first thug said, unwilling to be considered a dunce. "It's your hourly check-in with NATO to let them know that you're a real part of their game, right?"

"Right," Neil Steiner said, holding back a smile. He'd sent his message many times, and still held out hope that someone there would get curious, bring in a cryptographer, break the code, and stop this madness somehow. He always ended his contact with the request for a confirm. The confirm had never come, and it did not come now.

Steiner knew that he had no choice. As soon as the Polish warship arrived and the KGB man supplied the missing part of the code, he, Neil Steiner, dedicated NATO employee until temptation seduced him, would be the primary triggerman for World War III.

Minya Stalin stood beside Captain Nils Bridevell and peered through the icy windshield at the revived storm.

THE ASSASSIN CONVENTION

The Russian agent was seething with anger: at the storm for returning, at himself for having become seasick, and at the fact that they were already cruising off the north coast of Rügen Island and had not seen a sign of the destroyer. His boyhood friend had made a promise, and Stalin expected him to keep it. The fact that Stalin had little patience with keeping promises he, himself, made never entered his mind.

"Are you certain of your bearings?" Stalin asked the captain for the tenth time.

"Dead certain," the captain said curtly. Money or no money, he was tired of having his expertise questioned. "Three miles to our right, dead south of us, is the northern coast of Rügen. I have cruised this same course back and forth twice now, from one end of the island to the other. My instruments and my abilities do not lie. If you want further proof, I will turn south and run right into the goddamned island."

"All right," Stalin said just as testily. "Why haven't we seen the ship that was supposed to pick up me and my friends?" At the mention of friends, his anger rose. That stupid Moroccan woman and that vapid Cuban general were still in their cabins, sick as dogs.

They didn't have the right stuff for such work, in his opinion.

"Perhaps it is because the ship is not coming to pick you up," Captain Bridevell said softly. If such were the case, he knew that he wouldn't get that hundred thousand dollars. Once the storm finally did let up for good, he'd be deep-sixed by this desperate trio.

"The ship is here," Stalin pronounced. "If we were on

the prescribed course, we would see it.''

''Begging your pardon,'' the Danish captain said through gritted teeth, ''but we *are* on course. One more reference to some navigational error and—''

''I see something!'' Erik, the first mate, cried out. He was gazing northeast with a pair of powerful binoculars. ''A light of some kind,'' he added.

Stalin snatched the glasses and looked in that direction. He could barely make out, through the falling snow, a green running light of a ship.

''Head that way,'' he ordered Bridevell, pointing toward the dim light.

The captain checked his compass and the direction in which the Russian was pointing. ''Three degrees port,'' he muttered to himself as he turned the wheel slightly.

The bow of the *Hanseatic Queen* literally tore across rolling waves, heading toward the light seen by the first mate and then by the Russian. The boat slowed noticeably.

''Give it more throttle,'' Stalin commanded.

''The *Hanseatic Queen* is not an 'it,' '' Captain Bridevell shot back. ''The *Hanseatic Queen* is a 'she,' and she is already at full throttle. Stop asking the impossible.'' The captain knew that he was trying the Russian's patience and possibly blowing his chances of collecting his money, or even of staying alive, but he couldn't help it. Something about the domineering man got under his skin.

''Are your running lights on?'' Stalin demanded to know. ''Don't you have any brighter lights on this tub? Do something or the ship will miss us in this damned storm.''

THE ASSASSIN CONVENTION

Well, the Russian had him there. Captain Bridevell smarted over the fact that the Russian had called his lovely boat a tub, but he knew that he should have hit his searchlights the moment Erik reported seeing something out there in the blackness. He hit all switches, and the *Hanseatic Queen* turned into something resembling a carnival ride. Such lights are common on all fishing boats in the Baltic, where fog and storms are frequent, and bright lights aplenty are needed to keep the boats from running into each other. Few of them were sophisticated enough, or prosperous enough, to afford radar.

If the little fishing boat had become something of a Christmas tree in the black storm, it was nothing in comparison to what happened next. Lights from the destroyer dead ahead burst through the gloom like an invader from another galaxy. Every snowflake turned into sparkling, glistening crystals of light.

The two vessels could not miss each other now.

Ten minutes later, Captain Nils Bridevell and his first mate were on their way northwest toward Copenhagen. The captain had lashed the wheel in place, and he was counting the great wad of money he had been given for this night's work. There was only twenty thousand dollars, and this infuriated Bridevell, but he knew there was nothing he could do about it.

Aboard the destroyer, two boyhood friends were embracing. Polish officers on the bridge averted their eyes to avoid seeing their captain cry with joy. The steely eyes of the man who was supposed to be his friend were dry. That man, the officers decided, was a friend to no one. He cared about no one but himself. And for this man, their captain had disobeyed direct orders, an act that could cause repercussions down through the ranks, reducing stripes and pay scales, perhaps even bringing disciplinary action.

But the Polish destroyer, with the Russian on the bridge with his friend the captain, and the pretty woman and the arrogant Cuban down below in the sick bay, was now on its way to intercept the small craft that was still heading toward the lighthouse at Point Lochsa.

The duty officers on the bridge had no idea why the lighthouse was so important or why the small craft from Denmark was heading there. They knew only that their captain had wasted valuable time waiting for and picking up three strange individuals, one of them a mean-eyed Russian.

If the storm let up, they believed, the night could yet be saved. Their ship would overtake the small craft and the destroyer's guns would blow it out of the water.

Instead of reductions in rank and pay, and even possibly prison, they would be heroes. With such thoughts, the throbbing of the ship's powerful engines became a soothing sound to all the officers on the bridge.

They didn't even mind the presence of the Russian who seemed, after all, to speak Polish rather well.

Captain Lars Norrstrom was cold sober and did not like the feeling. He couldn't recall the last time he had been this sober. Half drunk, he was the best captain in all of Scandinavia; even fully drunk, he was still at least as good as anyone. Sober, he could be the best fishing boat captain in all the world, but Lars Norrstrom did not think in global terms. He would rather be half drunk and be the best in his own area, and to hell with the rest of the world.

"Welcome back to the land of the living," Nick Carter said as he watched the big blond captain maneuver the *Little Mermaid* through the deep troughs and great peaks of roiling seas. He had been watching the captain through the long voyage and knew from experience when the man was finally over the aftereffects of all the wine he'd been drinking.

"If this is living," Lars Norrstrom said grumpily, "why did you bring me back from the dead? By Christ, how we have kept from being sent to the bottom of this damned sea is beyond me. Are you some kind of god with special powers, and have I been going along on your spell?"

"I'm nobody special," Carter said, his eyes trained on the blackness ahead. "Perhaps we're both just incredibly lucky."

Lars Norrstrom grunted, coughed, and then spat into a brass spittoon he kept at the base of the compass binnacle. He fished in his jacket pocket and took out a crumpled bag of tobacco. "If I can't have a drink, would it trouble your mind much if I took third best—a good chew?"

"Not at all," Carter said, chuckling in spite of the anxiety that was building as they drew nearer to the lighthouse. "Incidentally, since you skipped from first to third, I assume that sex is second best."

"Wrong, my friend," the big Dane said. "First comes sex, then the drink, then the tobacco. As for my boat, it is in a special category all by itself, better than all three I have just mentioned."

"If it gets us to Point Lochsa," Carter said with a nod, "I'll agree with you." He lit up one of his own cigarettes.

"It must get us there and back again," Captain Norrstrom said tightly. "I have no desire to live out my life in a Polish lighthouse. By the way, my friend, since I undertook this voyage because you had a gun to my belly, I never felt it was important to ask why we were going to Point Lochsa and back. Could you tell me now?"

"It's better that you don't know," Carter said. The captain glared at him but kept his grip on the wheel. The little boat chugged bravely through the riot the storm was making of the water.

Carter had given their arrival a great deal of thought, yet had not yet come up with exactly what he would do once he got there. He was certain that the lighthouse would be manned with a platoon of armed thugs imported from the States. The M.O. of Raina Missou never seemed to vary.

Added to the problem of assaulting a heavily guarded lighthouse, and preserving the life of at least one man inside that lighthouse was the unending storm that would make a landing next to impossible. Carter had toyed with the idea of using a couple of life jackets from the boat and jumping overboard to let the waves carry him to the base of the lighthouse. That, he decided, was out. If he didn't freeze in the water, he'd certainly be smashed to death on the rocks at the lighthouse's base. He hadn't seen Point Lochsa or the lighthouse, but he knew the northern coast of Poland from aerial photographs he once had to study. The coast, the tiny islands, and the points were piles of rocks and boulders.

Carter figured that the lighthouse had to have a docking

area for the delivery of provisions by boat. The land around the lighthouse was too rocky for an airstrip. In the storm, though, it would be impossible to dock the *Little Mermaid*, even with the best skipper in the world at the helm.

And Captain Lars Norrstrom, Carter knew, was not the best skipper in the world, drunk or sober. But he'd have to do it.

FIFTEEN

Scanning the blackness ahead with the captain's binoculars, Carter heard the first soft cough of the starboard engine that spelled trouble. He had been feeling better about this mission now, difficult as it was, because he felt that he was well ahead of Minya Stalin, Raina Missou, and General Julio Vasco. Also, once Captain Norrstrom got used to the idea of being sober and of having so much money in his pockets upon his return to Copenhagen, he had actually become pleasant.

There was a second soft cough from the starboard engine, and then a miss from the one on the port side.

"Don't tell me we're out of gas," Carter said, gazing at the captain.

"Plenty of fuel," the captain said, checking the gauges on the tanks. "In fact, too much fuel. We have taken water into the tanks."

The engines kept running, though, and soon the coughing and missing stopped. Carter breathed easier, and when he saw the flickering light ahead in the snow, he wanted to cheer. It was the lighthouse at Point Lochsa.

"There it is," he told Lars Norrstrom. "Your heading is perfect."

"Of course," Captain Lars Norrstrom replied. "You expected less?"

Carter kept the binoculars trained on the light that kept turning and turning, illuminating the snowflakes and making the whole miserable journey worth it.

"Can you dock this thing without tearing us all to bits?" he asked the captain, knowing what the answer would be.

"I can dock the *Little Mermaid* anywhere," Lars Norrstrom said confidently, "and under any conditions. Just move back and give me room."

They were still about a mile from the lighthouse. To Carter, it seemed like twenty as the heavy seas kept slamming against the bow and making the little fishing boat seem to stand still. Carter moved farther from the helm and watched as the captain maneuvered the *Little Mermaid* upwind from Point Lochsa. He would approach the docking area at the base of the lighthouse with the wind and the waves at his stern. It was not good strategy, but it was the only strategy.

As the fishing boat moved in a wide arc east of the lighthouse to take advantage of the wind direction, two things happened almost simultaneously that quickly deflated Nick Carter's newfound optimism.

The engines of the *Little Mermaid* coughed and died,

and through the binoculars, Carter saw the running lights of a ship. It had to be the Polish destroyer. It was approaching from the direction of Rügen Island, and it was cutting through the thirty-foot waves as if they didn't exist.

"I think we've had it, Captain," Carter told Norrstrom. "I'm sorry I got you into this mess."

Captain Norrstrom had also seen the lights of the Polish destroyer, but it didn't instill fear in him. It made him angry. He began working various dials on the illuminated instrument panel of the fishing boat.

"What mess?" he asked. "We are almost there. I will have both engines going in twenty seconds."

"How?"

"Easy," Captain Norrstrom explained. "You never heard of rollover? It's when the contents of fuel tanks are reversed, from top to bottom. Without rollover, all the gunk in diesel fuel would settle to the bottom and clog the lines to the engines. Water in the tanks also sinks to the bottom. I have now rolled it to the top. Watch."

He hit the starters and the engines sprang into life.

But Carter still felt uneasy. That destroyer was closing in fast, though it had to be three or four miles away. They might make it to the dock first, but the destroyer, on arrival, could blow them out of the water with its four-inch guns.

Meanwhile, Captain Lars Norrstrom was easing the *Little Mermaid* into position, revving and easing back on its engines, maneuvering the boat perfectly into place along the dock, overriding the constant thudding of waves against the bow. When the engines started to cough again, he hit the proper switches to commence rollover, and the big diesels purred and roared with immense power.

And then the unexpected happened. Carter had expected the destroyer to open fire on the boat as soon as it came into range and view. Instead, the Polish warship circled the lighthouse and eased up to the dock, bow to bow with the *Little Mermaid*.

Three passengers left the destroyer and made their way into the lighthouse.

Carter recognized them immediately: Raina Missou, Minya Stalin, and General Julio Vasco.

He had blown it, Carter thought. Even if he could make it to the lighthouse without being shot by someone on the destroyer, what then? He would face a locked door and an unknown quantity of guards with an unknown variety of weapons.

Carter's biggest question concerned the Polish warship: Why hadn't it fired when it first saw the fishing boat? Surely land-based radar had been tracking the boat as it entered Polish waters, and surely the destroyer had been ordered to intercept it. And now the destroyer bobbed at the dock and Carter could see no sign of an enemy task force being sent to take over the *Little Mermaid*.

The man from AXE decided that he had spent enough time pondering unanswerable questions. It was time for action.

"Where are you going?" Captain Norrstrom asked as Carter began putting on the captain's oversize foul-weather gear. "You're going to get yourself killed out there—and I'll never see the money you promised me! What are we doing here anyway?"

"You'll get your money," Carter assured him as he

buttoned up the collar and slipped the hood over his head. He had slid Wilhelmina and three gas bombs into the large pockets of the weatherproof parka, and had two more gas bombs in the oversize rubber booots. "Just stay here and sit tight. I'll be back in twenty minutes."

"Sure," Captain Norrstrom said mockingly, "and St. Nicholas will come down my smokestack with twenty-five thousand dollars after Polish soldiers fill you full of bullets. Look at the boat we're sitting next to. Christ, why did I bring you here?"

"Because," Carter said through the mouthhole of the wool ski mask he had pulled over his head, "my money—and my gun pointed at your gut—together were very persuasive."

With that, he left the bridge and clambered down the ladder to the wharf. He had to time the bobbing of the boat, held against the dock by the churning engines, so that his leap wouldn't be so high that he might break his legs. The starboard gunwale of the *Little Mermaid* was bobbing up and down so furiously that at one minute it was below dock level, and at another, far above it.

He approached the dark hulk of the Polish destroyer. The snow had not let up, and the wind was howling wickedly. He clutched Wilhelmina in his gloved fist.

Carter had gone less than fifty yards when he knew that his task had gone from the difficult to the impossible. A wide steel door in the side of the destroyer had been slid aside. Standing in the opening, peering down at the dock, were twenty men with automatic rifles. His only route to the lighthouse was directly below them where they could not fail to miss him.

Thinking swiftly, Carter gauged the distance from the

175

dock to the open doorway high on the side of the destroyer. If he could lob a couple of gas bombs up there, he would send that crew of sharpshooters sprawling on the deck, most if not all of them dead. It would buy him time to reach the lighthouse, get inside, and confront whatever surprises awaited him there.

Time, he knew, was running out. Although the plan called for a dawn shot, the conspirators would be in a hurry, knowing that their prime nemesis had, against all odds, tracked them to the lighthouse.

Carter decided on two gas bombs, primed and thrown simultaneously. He moved as close to the destroyer as he dared. He shoved the Luger back into his pocket, pulled the pins on the gas bombs, and hurled them as hard as he could at the open doorway.

The wind was too strong. The tiny dark pellets sailed halfway up to the doorway where the gunmen waited, then seemed to hover in space for a time. They fell harmlessly into the sea as the wind carried the lethal gas away.

Carter cursed angrily. The men in the open doorway hadn't spotted him yet, but they would. And soon.

Any minute now, a cruise missile would be fired into the heart of Russia, and the die would be cast.

Nick Carter cursed again, his voice carried away on the wind, following the gas from his two useless bombs.

The *Hanseatic Queen* moved without running lights through the stormy night. Captain Nils Bridevell, still angry that he had been cheated out of eighty thousand dollars, stood at the helm and kept asking his first mate if he could see any lights in the darkness ahead.

"Nothing, sir," Erik kept responding. "Nothing at all."

"I know they were going to Point Lochsa," Captain Bridevell snarled. "The Polish destroyer is bigger and faster and is probably there by now. But that goddamned Russian isn't going there just for the sea air. He'll stay there after the destroyer drops him off—why, I don't know. I want that son of a bitch, Erik. I'm going to put my hands around his neck and make him cough up those eighty thousand dollars. I risked my life and my boat for that money, and I'm going to get it from that bastard! Do you understand my anger, Erik?"

"I do, sir," Erik said. A hundred thousand American dollars was a lot of money. And maybe, Erik hoped, if he helped his captain get the man, he'd receive more than the two thousand he was promised. His captain, he knew now, could well afford it. Two thousand didn't seem like nearly enough now for what he was doing. "I understand your anger quite well, and I share it. I'd like to squeeze his neck too."

The captain laughed and moved the helm slightly to starboard. "I'm not a selfish man," he said. "When we have this man in our grasp, the whole crew can line up for a squeeze or a punch or a kick. What's—Erik, turn your binoculars a bit more to starboard. Is there something there?"

Erik followed the captain's pointing finger and saw the flickering beam of the lighthouse, then the running lights of the destroyer. Then he slowly panned the dock and saw the fishing boat.

"It's impossible," he said.

"What's impossible?" Captain Bridevell demanded.

"I know that boat," Erik said. "It is the only one like it on the entire Baltic. It's the *Little Mermaid*. It is Captain Lars Norrstrom's boat."

Captain Bridevell snatched the binoculars and saw what Erik had seen. He, too, was puzzled, but for his own reasons. He had wondered all along why the Russian, the beautiful woman, and the Cuban had wanted to meet the Polish destroyer and then go on to Point Lochsa. Hell, *he* could have taken them to Point Lochsa. And why was Lars here, with his little boat bow to bow with the big destroyer?

And then Captain Nils Bridevell, now within a half mile of the lighthouse, saw something that made his anger even greater.

"Take the helm," he told his first mate. "Keep the heading."

Bridevell steadied the binoculars as best he could and watched the deck of the destroyer. Each time the beam from the lighthouse swept around, he could see a group of armed men moving up toward the bow. *Christ*, he thought, *they're going to start shooting at Lars. They're going to kill my old friend*.

All the years of jealousy and contempt, born of competition in the fishing waters of the Baltic, disappeared. Lars Norrstrom was no longer a competitor and a drunk to boot, a discredit to his profession as a fishing boat captain.

Lars Norrstrom was a fellow Dane, in grave danger of being killed by Communist soldiers.

"Prepare the torpedo!" he snapped at Erik. "I'm going to sink that Polish ship!" When Erik hesitated, the captain shouted: "Do it now! That's an order!"

Thirty seconds later, while Nick Carter still hovered in the lee of the destroyer trying to figure how to get past the crowd of gunmen above, and while an armed party reached the bow of the destroyer and was preparing to open fire on the bridge of the bobbing little fishing boat below, a tremendous explosion rent the air.

Captain Nils Bridevell, who had served on Danish warships, knew just where to aim his torpedo. He struck the powder room where the four-inch shells were stored for the guns above. When those shells detonated along with the payload of the torpedo, the interior of the Polish destroyer was all but gutted.

Nick Carter felt the impact and was thrown against a wall of rocks across the dock. The men who had been crouched in the open doorway above all came tumbling out, many of them dead before they struck the stone dock. Carter recovered just in time to pick off two survivors who were heading for the lighthouse.

Aboard the *Little Mermaid*, Captain Lars Norrstrom was cursing a blue streak. The powerful explosion had blown out his windshield and laced his face with tiny shards of glass. He held his painful face and felt the warm blood ooze through his fingers, but he knew that he was not seriously injured—somehow his eyes were not hit— and that his precious boat had survived intact.

Minya Stalin, seated in a swivel chair beside Neil Steiner in a room halfway up the tall lighthouse, had been staring at the computer screen when the explosion came. As Carter had suspected, the KGB man had moved up the time of firing. Already, Steiner had punched in half the required code and had received the proper responses.

"What the hell was that?" Raina Missou asked from behind the two men. In the cramped quarters of the little room where the computer terminal had been installed, the Moroccan woman and the Cuban general had crowded around to watch the KGB man and the computer expert make the necessary moves to fire the cruise missile. With them were two of the gunmen who had been guarding Steiner. All had been fascinated by the screen on which the green letters and numbers appeared.

Raina Missou leaned down to peer through a tiny window in the stone wall of the lighthouse. The whole outdoors, it seemed, was illuminated by an orange glow. She could see fires blazing inside the big destroyer, and she could see a column of orange flame shooting up through the falling snow.

"The destroyer blew up!" she cried. "My God, it just blew up! We're stuck here in this godforsaken place!"

"Shut up!" Minya Stalin ordered as he dashed to the narrow window to see for himself. Yes, they were stuck here until he could figure a way out. Even more, his old friend the captain was most assuredly dead. And then Minya Stalin saw the fishing boat. "Damn that Carter!" he swore. "He came with the drunken captain we left behind. I knew I should have killed that big blond oaf before we left."

General Julio Vasco, who showed no interest in the display of pyrotechnics outside, buffed his nails against the lapel of his uniform and said, "If the drunken captain's boat is here, then we have a way out. If Carter is with him, as you say, we have only to kill the American and leave with the big Dane. What could be simpler?''

Minya Stalin and Raina Missou looked at the Cuban for a long time and did not answer. Yes, what could be simpler? But had the general forgotten how he got that hideous scar on his throat?

It was not, the KGB man and the golden-skinned woman knew, all that damned simple.

Carter recovered quickly from the stunning blow he had received when the explosion slammed him against the wall of rocks. He moved carefully past the smoldering, fiery wreck that had once been a sleek warship and located the door of the lighthouse. Light streamed out into the night, illuminating the still-falling snowflakes. The impact of the explosion had blown the door open. Carter followed the light, Wilhelmina clasped in his hand.

He moved out of the light and leaned against the stone wall, wanting to lob in two or three gas bombs but knowing that he couldn't. If he could possibly save Steiner, he would. If he determined that the cruise missile was about to be fired, he wouldn't hesitate, but he knew that it would take time for the necessary codes to clear. And he hoped that the mysterious explosion that had destroyed the Polish warship had slowed the plans of the people upstairs.

There was a little time, Carter thought; he would use it well.

Captain Nils Bridevell, proud of his boat and of his aim, headed the *Hanseatic Queen* northwest toward Copenhagen. The torpedo that his boat carried—and that many Danish fishing boats carried to ward off Russian trawlers and fishing boats that encroached on their territory—had done its job.

The captain had not received the full amount of money that had been promised him for this dangerous run, but he was leaving with the satisfaction of believing that he had killed the people who had double-crossed him and his crew.

The sight of that mighty destroyer going up like a Roman candle had been worth the trip.

Bridevell would never know the full ramifications of that explosion, but he was satisfied with the knowledge that he had totally disabled a Polish warship and, in all probability, had killed the trio that had so cheated him.

It would be a rough voyage back home, but a happy one. As for Lars Norrstrom, well, the big man had been in tight scrapes before and had escaped.

He would do it again.

Carter's patience paid off. One of the gunmen inside the lighthouse, concerned about the wind and snow that was streaming into the open door, decided to repair the damage.

Carter slipped his Luger into his pocket and snapped Hugo into his hand. He slipped up behind the guard, ran the stiletto across the man's throat, and watched the blood gush out and down the man's front. The man's weapon, propped against the staircase leading up through the lighthouse, was an AK-47.

The Killmaster waited until he was certain the guard

was dead, then dragged him beneath the spiral staircase. He checked the Russian-made automatic rifle, found it ready to fire, and started slowly up the stone steps.

He found a second guard in the small circular room on the next level. The man was peering through a tiny window at the burning destroyer. The sound of the storm outside had muffled Carter's footsteps. Carter moved like a shadow up behind the man and whacked him in the temple with the butt of the automatic rifle. Leaving nothing to chance, he cut the man's throat and left him to die on the stone floor.

It was different at the third level. Two guards lay on bunks in the cramped quarters. Carter waited in shadow and heard the beeping sounds of a computer keyboard from the level above. Time was of utmost importance now. The code was probably being punched in, proper responses were being fed back, and any minute now, the signal to fire a cruise missile from a NATO country would be given.

Once that happened, it didn't really matter if Carter succeeded in cleaning out the lighthouse. Time, at a premium to him now, would be meaningless—to the whole human race.

Carter made a bold decision. Although he preferred to work quietly and in secret until the last minute, he decided to let those at the level above know that they were not as safe as they thought. He raised the AK-47 and let fly with a rain of copper-sheathed bullets at the men lying on the bunks.

Both men were immediately awakened by the sound of Carter pulling back the firing mechanism. Both saw the rifle pointed their way and were reaching for their own weapons when the deadly rain came. The first man had half his head torn away. The second man felt a dull punching in his stomach. The noise of the AK-47 firing in that small enclosed space was ear-splitting.

The results were what the Killmaster expected. He heard shouts from above. He heard chairs scraping. He heard footsteps moving in panic.

He called out, "Steiner! Your wife and children are safe! I have a note from Helen! She, Peter, Jan, and Lisette are safe in Paris! If you haven't punched in all the code, stop now! You'll be exonerated because of circumstances."

The result that Carter hoped for came swiftly. Steiner, certain that the man below was telling the truth, surprised everyone around him by leaping from his chair at the computer terminal and fairly falling down the steep stone steps. Carter caught him before he slammed into the floor.

He quickly pulled the pins of two gas bombs, heaved them up the stairs, and yanked a stunned Neil Steiner after him as he headed down through the lighthouse.

Captain Lars Norrstrom and the *Little Mermaid* waited, engines purring smoothly.

"What the hell happened in there?" Norrstrom asked Carter. He'd heard the shots. "Are you ever going to tell me what this is all about?"

"Later," Carter gasped. "Let's clear out for home!"

Once the boat moved away from the lighthouse, Carter explained a little of what had happened and of what they had prevented. Lars Norrstrom listened, fascinated.

"I know who sunk the destroyer," he said to Carter.

"It had to be whatever captain they hired to take them there. Why he did it, I don't know. Well, if he can torpedo a destroyer, I can torpedo a lighthouse and make sure those people never cause trouble again."

With that, he maneuvered the boat south of the burning destroyer, and after lining up with a spot where the base of the lighthouse met the sea, he punched a button. Something long and slender leaped from near the bow of the boat, causing the *Little Mermaid* to shudder.

The torpedo ripped into stone and sent a column of flame up through the lighthouse at Point Lochsa.

"Now," Captain Lars Norrstrom said with a wide smile, "if your friends are still alive after that, you might as well give up. You are dealing with demons from hell and not human beings. I don't know who you are, mister, but I think your troubles from that bunch are over."

Carter watched the flames that glowed from the site of the lighthouse. The building, and everything and everyone in it, was now a charred pile of rubble.

Carter sighed with relief and exhaustion. Soon they would be back in Copenhagen. Then he would return to Paris to Giselle, and Steiner would be reunited with his family. With the hypnotic throbbing of the twin diesel engines of the *Little Mermaid* in his ears and the image of the lovely Frenchwoman in his mind, Carter fell asleep where he sat. For the first time in almost two days, being out in the cold, the snow, and the driving wind didn't bother him a bit.

In his dream he was in a warm bed on Avenue St. Cloud, and he was enjoying every minute.

DON'T MISS THE NEXT NEW NICK CARTER SPY THRILLER

BLOOD OF THE SCIMITAR

It was about forty yards to the gate. Halfway there, the one on the wall spotted them and called down that he wanted cigarettes.

Carter looked up, shrugged both his shoulders, and lifted his arms in the air.

The guard on the wall cursed and resumed his pacing, walking away from them.

They went on and, without pausing, stepped through the narrow opening in the larger wooden gate.

The sentry had watched them, keen-eyed, all the way up to the gate and through it. Carter had watched his eyes and didn't like what he saw.

Suddenly there was a growled command from behind them that sounded like "Halt!" in any language.

"That's it," Rachel hissed, already rolling to the side. "I'll take the one on the wall."

Carter hit the ground, firing with the Stechkin on full automatic. The first two slugs caught wood. He sprayed, and the next five stitched the sentry across the middle.

The man fell back into the courtyard in a heap without firing a shot.

Rachel did as well, only not quite as clean. Her first burst caught the one on the wall in the legs. They went out from under him and he went airborne, screaming his lungs out in pain.

She silenced the screaming in midair with another burst.

"Let's go!" Carter rasped.

The town was like a hundred others in the Middle East and North Africa. Ramshackle, earth-colored huts sat crablike in an uneven line along dusty streets. They seemed to go on forever, until suddenly they came to an abrupt halt and then there was nothing but desert.

Carter spotted the minaret of the mosque, and motioned. Rachel nodded and charged in a new direction on yet another dark, quiet street.

They could hear yelling far behind them and exchanged looks as they ran.

"Let's hope," she gasped, "that they think it's an attack from outside and stay inside for a few minutes."

"My thoughts exactly!"

Another quarter mile, and the houses began to peter out. They jogged through a grove of date palms, then skidded to a halt.

About three hundred yards away was the small mosque and, just behind it, the helicopter, its lights burning.

Carter checked the terrain and, at the same time, calculated the time in his head.

To their left was a stream, probably not deep, but moving swiftly. To their right were the desert dunes rolling into infinity.

Around the helicopter were four guards, all alert now because of the firing.

"We've got to get them away from the chopper," Carter said. "One stray shot and there goes our transportation."

"I think I know how," Rachel said, starting to move toward them.

Before Carter could reply, she had gone back through the trees and into the darkness.

Carter fell to his belly and started moving across the sand. He had gone about fifty yards, when the whole world behind him exploded.

He rolled to his back and saw a fireball head for the heavens. It was huge, as big around as a football stadium, and trailing fire like the tail of a comet clear to the ground.

A figure all in white ran from the mosque.

Kassier.

Carter knew that the sheik's first thought, even before discovering the nature of the blast, would be to save his own skin.

Firing from such a distance wouldn't hit the chopper, even with the Stechkin.

He would have to rush them.

He was on his feet and running, his finger tightening on the trigger, when he heard the steady pounding of hoof-beats from his right.

He looked, and saw Rachel charging on a gray Arabian. She had thrown the burnoose back from her head, and her face and long flowing hair were revealed in the blazing light from the burning prison.

Kassier and the others around the helicopter saw her at the same time.

One of the men raised his rifle, but it was quickly knocked down by Kassier. He still wanted her alive.

All their attention was diverted now, and Carter broke into a sprint. He cut left just before the mosque, then right again along the stream.

Just before he went behind the building, he saw two of Kassier's soldiers throw their arms around the neck of Rachel's horse. A third was trying to pull her out of the saddle, and was getting his eyes gouged for his trouble.

Carter cleared the rear of the mosque and moved toward the copter in its shadows.

One man lay on the ground, digging at his eyes with his fingers and howling in agony. Another was nearby, gasping out his last breath. The Fiarbairon-Sykes was sticking out of his neck.

The two remaining soldiers held Rachel as Kassier stood in front of her yelling curses and questions.

The gist of her answers was that Carter had died trying to escape. She had set off a bomb in the prison and he had not got out.

Kassier seemed to accept this, but he did a lot more cursing, mostly at his own soldiers.

By this time, Carter had circled until he was on the blind side of the copter. He stayed out of the arcing light and crawled under the machine on his belly.

The pilot was still in the machine. He had probably started it on Kassier's orders when the armory blew. The sheik's first thought had probably been that they were under attack. Then, when he had spotted Rachel, he had probably figured out the real scam and halted his flight.

Now the rotor was churning up so much brush, sand and debris that Carter had no fear of being spotted.

Suddenly the engine and rotor idled down and he could hear Kassier's shrieking voice. Then one of the guards let go of Rachel and started sprinting up the road toward the source of noise and light.

From the look of it, the fire at the prison was spreading. Carter could hear the cries of civilians, and in the distance he could see people running every which way.

Kassier was backing toward the side of the copter and motioning the guard to bring Rachel.

Closer, Carter thought, *just a little closer* . . . .

He had slung the machine pistol over his back and now held the commando knife ready in his right hand.

For each backward step the sheik took, Carter pushed his knees further under him and lifted his butt higher in the air.

And then he was close enough.

The Killmaster was on him like a cat. Left arm under left arm, lifting, and around the throat beneath the chin. Right arm under right arm, knife point at the exposed column of the throat.

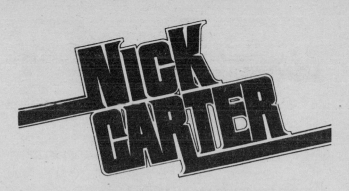

☐ 74965-8	**SAN JUAN INFERNO**	$2.50
☐ 14222-2	**DEATH HAND PLAY**	$2.50
☐ 45520-4	**THE KREMLIN KILL**	$2.50
☐ 52276-9	**THE MAYAN CONNECTION**	$2.50
☐ 06861-8	**THE BLUE ICE AFFAIR**	$2.50
☐ 51353-0	**THE MACAO MASSACRE**	$2.50
☐ 69180-3	**PURSUIT OF THE EAGLE**	$2.50
☐ 24089-5	**LAST FLIGHT TO MOSCOW**	$2.50
☐ 86129-6	**THE VENGEANCE GAME**	$2.50
☐ 58612-0	**THE NORMANDY CODE**	$2.50
☐ 88568-3	**ZERO-HOUR STRIKE FORCE**	$2.50

Prices may be slightly higher in Canada.

Available at your local bookstore or return this form to:

 CHARTER BOOKS
Book Mailing Service
P.O. Box 690, Rockville Centre, NY 11571

Please send me the titles checked above. I enclose _____ . Include 75¢ for postage
and handling if one book is ordered; 25¢ per book for two or more not to exceed
$1.75. California, Illinois, New York and Tennessee residents please add sales tax.

NAME_____

ADDRESS_____

CITY_____STATE/ZIP_____

(allow six weeks for delivery.)   A8

Bestselling Books

- [ ] 16663-6 **DRAGON STAR** Olivia O'Neill $2.95
- [ ] 08950-X **THE BUTCHER'S BOY** Thomas Perry $2.95
- [ ] 65366-9 **THE PATRIACH** Chaim Bermant $3.25
- [ ] 70885-4 **REBEL IN HIS ARMS** Francine Rivers $3.50
- [ ] 02572-2 **THE APOCALYPSE BRIGADE** Alfred Coppel $3.50
- [ ] 65219-0 **PASSAGE TO GLORY** Robin Leigh Smith $3.50
- [ ] 75887-8 **SENSEI** David Charney $3.50
- [ ] 05285-1 **BED REST** Rita Kashner $3.25
- [ ] 75700-6 **SEASON OF THE STRANGLER** Madison Jones $2.95
- [ ] 28929-0 **THE GIRLS IN THE NEWSROOM** Marjorie Margolis $3.50
- [ ] 87127-5 **WALK ON GLASS** Lisa Robinson $3.50
- [ ] 25312-1 **FRIENDS IN HIGH PLACES** John Weitz $3.50
- [ ] 11726-0 **A CONTROLLING INTEREST** Peter Engel $3.50
- [ ] 02884-5 **ARCHANGEL** Gerald Seymour $3.50

Bestselling Books from Berkley – action-packed for a great read

___ \$3.95 07657-1 **DAI-SHO** Marc Olden

___ \$3.50 07324-6 **DAU** Ed Dodge

___ \$3.95 08002-1 **DUNE** Frank Herbert

___ \$3.95 08158-3 **RED SQUARE** Edward Topol and Fridrikh Neznansky

___ \$3.95 07019-0 **THE SEDUCTION OF PETER S.** Lawrence Sanders

___ \$4.50 07652-0 **DYNASTY: THE NEW YORK YANKEES 1949 – 1964** Peter Golenbock

___ \$3.95 07197-9 **THE WORLD WAR II QUIZ AND FACT BOOK** Timothy B. Benford

___ \$2.95 06391-7 **JOURNEY INTO FEAR** Eric Ambler

___ \$2.95 07060-3 **THE KHUFRA RUN** Jack Higgins writing as James Graham

___ \$3.50 06424-7 **SCARFACE** Paul Monette

___ \$3.50 07372-6 **THE BILLION DOLLAR BRAIN** Len Deighton

___ \$4.50 07664-4 **INFAMY: PEARL HARBOR AND ITS AFTERMATH** John Toland

___ \$3.50 06534-0 **THE KILLING ZONE: MY LIFE IN THE VIETNAM WAR** Frederick Downs

Prices may be slightly higher in Canada.